SCOTT PHILLIPS

THE ADJUSTMENT

A NOVEL

COUNTERPOINT

Library of Congress Cataloging-in-Publication Data

Phillips, Scott.
  The adjustment :
a novel / Scott Phillips.
    p. cm.
  ISBN 978-1-58243-730-9
  1. Veterans—Fiction. 2. Wichita (Kan.)—Fiction. I. Title.

  PS3566.H515A66 2011
  813'.54—dc22

                          2011005413

Cover design by Michael Fusco
Interior design by www.meganjonesdesign.com
Printed in the United States of America

COUNTERPOINT
1919 Fifth Street
Berkeley, CA 94710

www.counterpointpress.com

Distributed by Publishers Group West
10 9 8 7 6 5 4 3 2 1

THE ADJUSTMENT

ONE
THE
FUNNY PAGES

WHEN I GOT home at five and told Sally I was heading for Kansas City, she blew right up and wanted to know where the hell I got off just taking off without any advance warning.

We'd been married for a long time—since '39—but the war came along and I was gone so long I really had halfway forgotten I was someone's husband. I'd actually been less accountable when I was in the army, having only a corrupt first looey to answer to instead of a wife and an employer.

"Listen up. This is my job, and unless you want to get one yourself I need to keep it. And when the old man says jump, I jump."

I closed my suitcase and tried to kiss her, and she pulled back. I laughed and lunged for her, caught her by the shoulders and pulled her close. She relaxed and kissed me back, and I was starting to wish I could put off my departure by an hour or so.

"Just tell the old man to give you a little more advance notice next time. I had a nice dinner planned." Her pretty pout turned into a beautiful half smile, and I swatted her on the ass on my way to the front door.

I HEADED NORTH in my company Olds to Seventeenth and headed east past Wichita U, where I'd spent four years studying business and trying to screw coeds when Sally wasn't looking, and wondered idly about going back nights for a master's degree. For the moment I was enjoying my work at Collins Aircraft well enough, but who knew, it might get tired. Right now it was hard to imagine doing any one thing for the rest of my life, even though I knew that I was going to have to pick something before too long.

I turned onto Oliver and then onto Thirteenth, where I was surprised to see some signs of development; this far northeast had seemed destined to be farmland forever. Like all the other changes Wichita had undergone in my absence I took it as almost a personal affront, something that had been done just to disorient me when I got back.

The sun was already down, and it was cold as a well digger's ass, and right then it started to snow. I cursed and turned on the wipers; if it was slick all the way to KC it would add an hour or more to the trip.

NOT THAT IT really mattered. The truth was I could have spent the night in Wichita and made the trip early the next morning. But there was something I wanted to do that night if I could arrange it, and an extra night away from Wichita was always cause for celebration, even if it meant pissing off my beautiful, mercurial Sally.

IT WAS ALMOST midnight when I hit Kansas City, and a quarter past when I stepped inside Drake's, an all-night diner catering to employees of St. Luke's hospital. The woman I wanted to see didn't get off until three in the morning, but if I read the *Star* and the *Times* both right down to the classifieds I could keep myself occupied until she got home to let me in.

At the counter I ordered coffee and eggs. The *Star* led with the murder-suicide of a married couple in tony Overland Park, the twist being that the wife had done the shooting. Their grown daughter, other relatives, and longtime family friends all proclaimed their bafflement; the deceased had no known health or marital problems, and they'd planned to mark their twenty-fifth wedding anniversary two months hence with a party that had been anticipated as one of the highlights of Kansas City's social season. Hubby was a reserve officer in the Army Air Corps and had flown missions over Germany, the article said, and had been back about as long as I had.

On an inside page was a nice photo of the murder house, a vast Tudor with a palatial lawn and circular drive. "*The Harold J. Lamburton residence, scene Friday of the shotgun murder of Mr. Lamburton and the suicide of his wife, the former Christine Whittaker. Star File Photo.*" That's high society, when the paper keeps a file picture of your house. I wondered if she used a rabbit gun for better coverage, or something bigger calling for greater accuracy; a lot of girls in that part of the country were handy with a shotgun, even—maybe especially—in that rarified social stratum.

"You want more coffee?" the counterman asked, tapping the portraits of the dead. "Lady was fucking the Fuller Brush man while he was away is what I think. He found out about it and she killed him."

"Fuller Brush men take a Christian oath not to fuck housewives."

"Milkman, gardener, eggman, I don't know. One of 'em." He had a very distracting deformative growth on the left side of his nose that made his whole face look lopsided. It had almost the exact texture and color of a cauliflower, with several thick black hairs curling outward from it. This, I'm guessing, was why he was stuck on the overnight shift. "All's I know is after a while a wife gets restless with a man gone. You see that picture of the two of 'em?"

I reopened the *Star* to page four for another look at their portraits. Harold was a burly, round-faced man with the look of a petty tyrant, whereas Christine, looking a good deal younger than her forty-eight years, beamed forth from her photo with the enthusiastic smile of a girl. It was easy to picture her as a flapper right out of John Held, Jr., and just as easy to picture that same girl waking up one morning twenty-five years on and, upon finding herself married to Wallace Beery, trying to work out where he'd hidden the key to the gun closet.

"She ain't hard to look at, for a gal her age, is all I'm saying," the counterman said. "I'd've fucked her." He pulled the paper close to that cauliflower tumor, squinting. "Look how popeyed she is, though. Maybe she was hooked on pep pills. Those people get all kinds of crazy ideas in their heads."

An old man came in, shuffling and wheezing, and joined in the discussion; his son had known the murdered man slightly. "Cruel man, Lamburton. Wouldn't let her travel to see her mother once, for instance, when the old lady was sick. I expect it only got worse after he'd been gone a while." He took off his scarf and his thick woolen overcoat and ordered a bowl of chili, which he proceeded to slurp like a small child. Coat off, he was revealed as a tall man bent over rather than a short heavyset one; his hands were enormous, hammy, broken-knuckled things, so dry there were cracks at the joints, filled in with dried blood like blackened spackle.

After a while a gaunt young man in a white coat came in and ordered coffee and eggs, followed by a couple of middle-aged women with their nurse's caps still on. At ten after three I sauntered down to where Broadway turns into Nichols Parkway. After ten minutes sitting in the cold on the stoop of Vickie's building she showed up, looking good for a woman who'd just wrapped up a ten hour shift of waking people up for shots and getting ordered around by twenty-five-year-old interns. She put her finger up to her lip to keep me quiet and opened her front door. Once inside she turned on a lamp and shut the door; it was still pretty dark in there, with her walls painted a curious mallard green.

"Wasn't expecting to see you anytime soon, Wayne."

"Unexpected business trip, just came up this afternoon. Thought I'd look you up."

"Lucky me, I guess."

We necked for a minute, then started dancing towards the back of the apartment where the bedroom was. Then she stopped me and pointed to the couch.

"Sit down for a minute, I got something to show you before we go any further."

I did as I was told and after a few seconds' rustling around in the bedroom she came back out holding a folded sheet of Armed Services stationery, which she stuck into my hand.

"I want you to read this before we get started, Wayne," she said, and then she went into the kitchen.

The letter was from her husband, an Army MD who claimed to have seen some awful things before the peace. Now he was in Vienna in the American sector taking care not just of our own but the Krauts as well, in particular their malnourished orphan children. The Captain tended toward the purple end of the epistolary spectrum, both in describing the rickety tots in his care and in his choice of endearments, and the whole thing smelled to me of rosewater and horseshit. At "Eternally, your Jeffrey" I rolled my eyes skyward one last time, folded the thing up, and called her back in.

"So?" I said.

"Does it bother you, knowing you're cuckolding Dr. Schweitzer?"

"Not particularly," I said.

"Okay." She gave me a funny, quizzical look, as if that wasn't exactly the answer she was expecting.

"How long after you got married did he ship out?"

"Right after."

Getting hitched was his idea, I guessed, the idea being to keep her on the hook while he was gone, but I didn't say it. "If you're feeling bad about it . . . "

"I know, I know, he's probably bedded down with a dozen grateful Kraut widows after he vaccinated their kids." She snatched the letter out of my hand. "I just thought you ought to have an idea who you're messing with is all."

Then she grinned and stood facing me, hands on her hips, tits thrust forward. "You want to try and take my uniform off, smart guy?" she said, and I started peeling away her stiff whites piece by piece, with their arousing starch smell.

I knew exactly who I was messing with.

MUCH LATER IN the dark as I lay there listening to the radiator popping, she startled me by saying quietly, "Wayne? You asleep?"

"Nope."

"How'd you get the scar?"

"Which scar?"

"You know which."

It wouldn't do to tell her the truth. Broadminded though she was, "stabbed by a rival pimp in Rome" wasn't going to score me any points romantically, so I said "Iwo Jima."

"I happen to know you spent the whole war in Europe," she said, but she didn't press the point, and after a while we went to sleep.

AT ELEVEN IN the morning we strolled over to Drake's for breakfast. The man with the cauliflower nose was gone, replaced by a funereal chain smoker who made a show of letting his ash extend out over the grill until the last possible moment, at which point he tapped it onto the floor.

The Sunday *Star* had a rehash of yesterday's murder without much new information, but with some illuminating photos from the society files of the unfortunate couple at various charity events. One of them seemed chosen specifically for the enervated dementia in Christine Lamburton's eyes as she stood in a semicircle of worn-out former debs honoring themselves for rolling bandages during the war, or some such laudable sacrifice. Nutty as Mrs. Lamburton looked in that picture, I recognized it as the kind of crazy that can seem like a whole lot of fun at first, before the scary kicks in; late in the game had the old boy ever seen that cockeyed glint and worried, just a little, for his life?

Victoria's appetite was healthy and she managed an entire plate of corned beef hash and three fried eggs, and I settled for Cream of Wheat with a side of bacon. Afterwards we walked down Broadway to where my car was parked and I kissed her goodbye. I was about to pull away from the curb when she knocked on the window, opened the door, and slid in beside me.

"When are you coming back next?"

"Don't know," I said. "Hard to know when I'll be free for a couple days."

"Let me know in advance next time. I'll take some time off." She kissed me again, the taste of her mouth a pleasant mix of coffee and corned beef and Doublemint, and then she slid out of the car and walked carefully back up the icy pavement to her building.

DOCTOR BECK OWNED an apartment building on Troost off of Van Brunt, one of those places with a big staircase up the middle and three floors of apartments on either side. He kept one apartment on the first floor for his own use, and I wondered what the other tenants made of their occasional short-term neighbors, sad young women moving in for a week or so and then moving on to their other distant lives. I suppose in between those brief tenancies the doctor must have entertained women there himself.

The girl I was picking up today was a stranger to me, the first I'd chauffeured back to Wichita under similar circumstances since before the war. She was skinny and sniffly and peaked, and she didn't say anything when Beck gave her last-minute instructions for the coming few days. She didn't speak until we got down to Emporia, about halfway to Wichita, and that was just to express a desire to go to the bathroom.

"You want something to eat?"

"I don't have any cash on me," she said as I pulled off onto Telegraph Street.

"You don't need cash," I said.

SHE NIBBLED AT a grilled cheese sandwich and wouldn't meet my eyes. The waitress gave me a nasty look, though, like I was the one who'd made the girl miserable. She had mousy brown hair and acne, and I sat wondering what the hell old man Collins had been thinking.

"What's your name?" I asked her, finally.

"Emily," she said.

"You have a job, Emily?"

"I was in the steno pool at Collins." She sneaked a quick glance at my face.

"You were?"

"I was fired after . . . " She took a long time swallowing a bite of her sandwich. "They let me go when I got in trouble."

"Is that so."

She looked me square in the face now, puzzled. "Uh-huh."

"Girly, they can't fire you."

"Sure they can." Her eyes were wet and her voice quavering but she wasn't giving in to it yet. "It's in the employee manual, about moral turpitude."

"Doesn't mean a damned thing. You've got the great man over a barrel."

So I laid it out for poor Emily: in a couple of days she was to call Mr. Collins's personal secretary, Miss Grau, and tell her that a man named Hiram Fish has been pestering her, trying to find out where she'd been and why she wasn't employed by the company any more.

"Who's this man Fish?"

"Someone Mrs. Collins uses to keep up on Mr. Collins's comings and goings."

"And what does Miss Grau do after I tell her this?"

"Miss Grau gets you your job back, with a raise if you look like you're not sure you want it back."

"I'm not sure I do," she said, but I noticed she was eating the second half of her grilled cheese with gusto.

"A job at Beechcraft or Cessna, then. Listen, you think all he owes you is a trip to KC and a grilled cheese sandwich? Take it from me, a lot of girls have been in your situation, and some of them ended up better off than others."

I didn't give two shits about the dim bulb across the booth from me, but I got a hell of a kick out of fucking with my employer and her impregnator, Everett Collins. Aviation pioneer, friend to Wiley Post and Lucky Lindy, founder of one of the nation's biggest aircraft plants, a bigger man himself than anyone in Wichita had ever thought about being. He'd been my childhood hero, which may go some way to explaining the depth of my current contempt for the man.

TWO
RUTH SNYDER'S
PRETTY ANKLES

I F YOU ARE a reasonably competent and ambitious individual with
a bit of initiative and creativity, and a willingness to look at strict
regulations as loose guidelines to be skirted when necessary or conve
nient, there is no better job for you than Master Sergeant in the United
States Army Quartermaster Corps.

I volunteered in December of '41, and like everybody else my
motives at that time were strictly patriotic, although a certain desire to
escape the wife and hometown for a while did play a minor role. My
wife Sally was all for it, and proud as hell of me. The objection came
from Everett Collins; back then Collins was less of a lunatic, and I was
actually touched at his concern for me, though I see it in retrospect as
petulance at the loss of a useful subordinate.

Getting assigned to the QM Corps was the single best stroke of
luck in my life. At first I objected to it because of the fact that the Corps
kept its men behind the lines; I wanted to kill Nazis with my bare

hands or, failing that, a rifle. But before long I started getting reports back from the front, and I realized that my job as Quartermaster was probably going to keep me alive for the duration.

By the time I was reassigned to Rome from London I was an old hand at thievery and black marketeering, and I had some small experience as a pimp as well, though the possibilities there far exceeded what I could accomplish in old Blighty, where the systems of local vice remained more or less intact during the conflict; Rome's had been shattered by the war and the fall of the fascists.

And now I was back in my hometown, with a wife who looked like a movie star and a job that entailed more boozing and carousing than actual work. What the hell was the matter with me that I was missing the excitement and danger of the war? Granted, the dangers I'd faced were nothing compared to those experienced by the troops at the front, but I did have that scar from being stabbed, and I was shot at more than once by unsatisfied johns and once was threatened by a purchaser of black market gasoline who wanted the stuff for free. A colleague of mine made sure he didn't come around any more, and I never knew exactly what happened, but I have a suspicion that the answer lies at the bottom of the Tiber.

It was a Thursday, and I was looking at the *Evening Beacon* in Red's, a roadhouse five miles east of the Wichita city limit on 54. You could do a fair number of theoretically illegal things at Red's, as long as you knew how to ask and didn't make a spectacle of yourself. Kansas was a dry state, and if you wanted anything stronger than 3.2 percent beer, you had to go across state lines or to a blind pig or to a roadhouse like Red's, whose owner paid the authorities well to look the other way.

There was an interesting article in the *Beacon* about a foot somebody found underneath a bridge in Riverside. It was a man's right foot, the article said, size eleven, and there was a pretty good quote from the elderly fisherman who found it: "I hate to think of somebody gimping around missing a foot."

The *Beacon* was a better read than the rival *Eagle* if you were looking for sex and mayhem. When a car hit a train, the *Eagle* would report the casualties but the *Beacon* would be there with a photographer to record the blood and guts and tortured metal, and I felt sure the *Beacon*'s editors were bitterly disappointed at their failure to get a picture of the foot.

"How's that pretty wife of yours," Everett Collins asked me, one elbow on the bar, annoyed that I was reading the paper instead of listening to him.

"Same as ever," I said. The fact that he wanted so badly to screw my dear Sally was one of several things that kept me employed and relatively free of actual day to day responsibility. "How's yours?"

He stared at me for a second like he was going to lose his temper, then he laughed, just drunk enough to find my impertinence funny. I couldn't have imagined needling the boss before the war, but I wasn't scared of him any more. He slapped his palm down on the bar. One of his ears was missing its lobe, having been sliced off in some long-ago cutting scrape he never elaborated on, and that ear always got redder than the other when he got mad or drunk.

"Thinks she's going to outlive me. When I croak, you make sure the cops take a real good look at her. I got it in my will if I die before she does I want a full autopsy."

"I'll see that she gets the chair whether she's guilty or not."

He laughed again. "I like that. Maybe I should just have her framed for something while I'm still kicking, then I'd get to watch her burn. You ever see that picture of Ruth Snyder in the chair?"

"No."

"Some reporter snuck a camera into the witnesses' gallery, strapped it to his shin, snapped one right when they turned on the juice. Kind of blurry. Strapped into that chair with a hood over her head, body all tensed up with the current running through her."

"Never saw that."

"January '28. I was in New York talking to the bankers the day it ran, took up the whole the front page of the *Daily News* and I tell you what boy, I had to have a call girl sent up to my room so I didn't walk into those bankers' offices with a goddamn hard-on."

At times like these I almost liked him. Hung over, which was as close as he got to sober any more, he was a surly mean son of a bitch, and much drunker than this he'd be pissing his pants and throwing wild punches, protected by his money and his power in these parts as much as by the presence of Billy Clark, the ex-cop who followed him around most nights to make sure he got home in one piece.

It was only seven o'clock, and I guessed Billy had another seven or eight hours to go. The bartender, an old-before-his-time hillbilly named Jake Bearden with eyebrows like blond sagebrush and deep furrows running from his nose alongside his mouth, looked like he wanted to say something but he kept his counsel.

"I think I'd like to get me some strange tonight, Wayne," the old man said.

What he meant was I should pick up some girls and he'd decide which one he wanted to screw. Looking around the roadhouse I saw only two unaccompanied women, both of them worn-out b-girls the old man had tired of months before. "Pickings are slim around here," I said as one of the girls, thinking herself unnoticed, delicately stuck her little finger up a nostril and, upon extraction, examined the nail with a curiosity as dull as her blonde permanent.

"Why don't you call one of your friends and get some fresh gals out here."

"Management doesn't like that." Red Garnett, the roadhouse's owner, had warned Collins not to bring any more whores around, at least not in the numbers the old man liked. Last time the unpicked extra girls went around propositioning the other customers and while this wasn't necessarily bad for business, it wasn't covered under the terms of his deal with the county. Liquor and gambling were all old Red could afford to pay off, and he'd warned me more than once that the slack he'd been cutting the old man was not unlimited.

"Let's head out to the Eaton and get you a suite, and we can have some girls sent up," I said.

He scowled like a disappointed five-year-old. "All right." He picked his bottle up off the bar and headed for the door with me close behind. I waved at Billy Clark, and he climbed out of his booth, shaking his head.

On the way to the Eaton he pontificated about the natural states of men and women, and men's physical needs versus women's. It was one of his standard lectures, and I marveled that before the war I used to take his shit seriously, listening to his lame-brained theories and thinking how lucky I was to be able to bask in the presence of the Great Man. He had been good at one thing in his youth, putting airplanes together, back in the days when they were much simpler craft than they are now. Sure, he had to improvise and invent in those days, and I'll give him that much. But on any subject outside the mechanics of flying machines he was a fool and a blowhard.

BY THE TIME I got back to the apartment that night I'd paid off four girls, only two of whom ended up getting screwed in Collins's Packard. One of the others made a play for Billy, who turned her down flat, and I screwed the fourth in the parlor of the suite we'd rented. It was close to three when I opened the door and heard Sally's voice from the bedroom.

"Honey?"

"It's me."

"Want to come to bed?"

Having had the foresight to take a shower back at the suite, I was reasonably sure no traces of the whore's smell remained, but I'd still hoped to come home and find my wife asleep. When I pushed the bedroom door open I found her lying on the bed wearing nothing but her high heeled shoes and enough makeup to caulk a small bathroom, one long leg stretched out and the other raised up at the knee.

"I been awful lonesome tonight," she said.

I WAS A little sorry about the whore at the Eaton, because it took me a good half an hour to get to the point of ejaculation. Afterward we lay there staring at the ceiling and she started talking, babbling the way she did sometimes about babies and the meaning of life and marriage and church and all that kind of crap.

Now she was saying something that required a response, and having no idea what the subject at hand was, I let out a long, thoughtful sigh.

"I just think a child ought to have a yard to play in," she said.

"That's true." Jesus, what was she saying? That snapped me right back to attention.

"And a neighborhood where there are other children to play with."

Something vaguely electrical ran from the top of my head to the base of my spine. "Wait a second. What were you just saying a minute ago?"

She hit me with her pillow and started for the bathroom.

"You son of a bitch, you're not even listening to me!" She slammed the bathroom door shut behind her and started running a bath.

I knocked on the door. "I'm sure as hell listening now," I yelled, at which point the phone rang.

"Mr. Ogden? It's Mrs. Dunphy downstairs."

"Sorry, Mrs. Dunphy," I said, though I wasn't sorry in the least; I loathed the old termagant and her pasty husband. "We'll quiet down."

"You know perfectly well my Hank goes to work at six-thirty. This is not fair."

It suddenly struck me as funny that at this late stage of her dismal existence Mrs. Dunphy still expected things to be fair, and I was still laughing after she hung up on me.

THREE

A PALMFUL OF WARM SPIT

A FEW DAYS LATER I was still getting over the shock of having knocked up my wife. Sally had woken up nauseous and pissed off at me for something she couldn't or wouldn't put into words, and for the first time since my return in May I was missing the nature of my relations with the gals in my employ in Rome: sexual in several cases but strictly impersonal.

It was Monday morning and my first task of the day was to spring a couple of farmboys at Police Headquarters downtown. The clerk didn't ask me why I was bailing them out, just gave me the fisheye and breathed in and out with a loud, phlegmy sound while he filled out the forms and stamped the endorsement onto the back of the Collins Aircraft Company check. Considering the amount of time I spent watching and helping Everett Collins break various laws, the clerk and I probably ought to have been on a first name basis, but the great man couldn't get arrested in Wichita for anything short of manslaughter.

The clerk knew who I was, though, and he knew what the farmboys had done.

"Heard they busted his ribs. Heard Billy Clark wasn't much help to him, either. Some bodyguard."

"That's about right."

"You fixing to bail him out too?"

"I'm going to let Billy-boy cool his heels in the jug until he's arraigned. Let him do some thinking in there."

"Heard he told old man Collins he was retired from the force."

"Isn't he?"

"Hell, no. Fired, fall of '44. Pulled his service revolver on a civilian over at Lawrence Stadium, off-duty, before a ball game. Claimed it was a legit arrest, turned out to be a beef over a parking space. We hired a whole bunch of 4-F morons when our men started signing up and getting drafted, and that's one time it bit us right in the ass. Collins ought to have had him checked him out before he put him on the payroll."

ONCE THEY GOT out, the farmboys didn't show much curiosity as to who I was or why I'd posted their bail. A pair of giant brothers by the name of Gertzteig, they seemed to think this was just the way things worked in the big city. "Come on, I'll buy you breakfast."

We went across the street to the drugstore and sat down. "Anything you like, boys, it's on me."

A couple of uniformed officers were enjoying their complimentary breakfast at the other end of the lunch counter, and glancing at the brothers, they surely pegged them for the recently sprung drunks they were. Back at the pharmacy counter I could see the pale, baldheaded druggist staring daggers at the freeloading cops. He hated giving away those free meals, and locating his drug store across the street from City Hall turned out to be the worst mistake he'd ever made.

The Gertzteigs ordered up t-bones and fried eggs, sunny side up, and hash browns and toast, both of them, and they attacked the meals when they came in exactly the same order: potatoes, eggs, toast, steak. They weren't twins, as far as I could tell, but they matched each others' motions pretty well. I wouldn't have wanted to get into a fight with them, especially with a wobbly drunk like Collins on my side.

"So here's the deal, boys. You know the old man you hit?" I asked between mouthfuls of corned beef hash.

"Only hit the old guy but the one time," said the bigger of the two. "In the ribs."

"Once't was enough," said his brother.

"We wasn't mad at him so much, it was his friend."

"The old man feels bad you spent the night in jail, and he wants to give you a little something to get home on." I handed them each an envelope containing a fifty dollar bill. Examining the contents they grew more slackjawed than before.

"Golly damn," said the bigger one. "That's purt square of a feller just lost a fight."

"He doesn't want you boys to walk away from Wichita thinking that's the way things usually go in the big city. Now can I give you boys a ride to wherever your car is so you can get on back to Butler County?"

I DIDN'T BOTHER phoning Collins to tell him about it. He'd grouse about the expense and indignity of having to pay off the cretins who'd broken two of his ribs, but in a day or two he'd see the logic of it, and he'd be as grateful as I was for the knowledge that the Gertzteig brothers had no idea of the identity of their assailant-turned-benefactor. And my next task was unpleasant enough without Collins making it worse. By ten AM Billy Clark had already been before the judge and released, and I called him on the phone and told him to meet me at Red's.

I WAS STASHING the receipt for the boys' bail in my inside overcoat pocket when I noticed an envelope I'd almost forgotten. It was addressed to WAYNE OGDON COLLINS AIRPLANE CO. WITCHATA KAS, and it had nonetheless managed to make its way to my desk a mere two weeks after someone mailed it from Salem, Massachusetts, a town I had never visited and from which no acquaintance of mine had, to my knowledge, ever sprung. I guess I'd had it sitting there in the pocket for a week or more, some irrational sense of dread having stopped me from opening it when I saw it laying there on top of some reports I didn't intend to read.

Inside was a penciled note, crudely printed in block letters:

YOU SON OF A BITCH THIEF THERES' BLOOD ON
YOUR HANDS. ERUOPEAN LADYS ARE DELICATE
AS FLOWERS.

Something went sour in my stomach, and I tried to put it down to the corned beef.

THAT NIGHT WE sat in Billy Clark's usual booth. It was another quiet night at Red's, but we were familiar enough from our visits with the old man that the b-girls didn't bother us, though one of them kept giving us cold, appraising looks that gave me the fantods. "What are we going to do about this?" I asked him.

"Don't know," he said. He had two black eyes and a split lower lip, and his right index finger was in a little metal splint wrapped with surgical tape.

"You should have told Mr. Collins when he hired you that you couldn't fight worth a damn."

"You didn't see them two farmboys that jumped us," he said.

"I sure did, I made their bail and paid 'em off and sent 'em back to Butler County. Now what the hell were you thinking starting a fight yourself? And don't try telling me anything different because I talked to three people who watched it."

"I don't know, Wayne. Something about them just set me off."

"Another thing. Mr. Collins knows about the incident that lost you your badge."

He reared back and craned his neck to look at the ceiling, a gesture meant to convey exasperation at the unfairness of the thing that instead suggested an inability to meet my eyes. "That business was a bunch of lies from start to finish."

"Nonetheless Mr. Collins feels it would be best if you sought employment elsewhere."

His mouth hung open and his eyes watered as if I'd just slapped him. All he'd expected was a reprimand. I was tired of looking at Billy, though, and I didn't like his lying, and he'd proved that as a bodyguard he was useless. I handed him a check on Collins's personal account. "Two weeks severance and you're lucky to get it."

COLLINS HAD TAKEN to phoning me at home, a familiarity I was beginning to resent but hadn't yet figured out how to stymie. That night when he called I told him I'd fired Billy. Might as well take the hit now if he was going to react badly.

There was a long pause on the other end of the line, complete with tightly controlled breathing. "Son of a bitch had some balls calling himself a bodyguard. Put an ad in the paper for somebody new."

"Already set for tomorrow's *Beacon*."

"Shit. That Jew rag? Put one in the *Eagle* instead. Nobody reads the *Beacon* but left-wing degenerates."

This I would ignore. I liked the busty girl who ran the *Beacon*'s classified desk. "Anything else?"

"Yeah. Come on over and see if you can't sneak some booze in. Bring a flask or two. Make it three. I can hide 'em; we'll tell the old bitch you're here to discuss advertising strategy."

THE AD IN the *Beacon* read as follows:

> *Man with police or military experience wanted for*
> *bodyguard work. Familiarity with firearms essential.*
> *References. Box 397, Beacon.*

The day after the notice first appeared I had half a dozen responses. One was a woman whose husband had taught her to use a rifle. Two were from ex-convicts who at least had the honesty to admit it. One was from Billy Clark, admirably already on the lookout for new opportunities. The two who remained were ex-servicemen, and I made arrangements to meet them both at Stanley's diner at Kellogg and Oliver.

The first was a barrel-chested ex-marine who sat across from me, seething over some unspecified grievance.

"How's civilian life agreeing with you?" I asked him.

"Bitch don't know when to quit."

"Yeah, ain't that the way."

"I swear to Christ, Mister, I know she was fucking my brother while I was gone."

A hell of a thing to say to a stranger in the context of a job interview, I thought; this guy needed his head shrunk more than he needed a job. "That's pretty rotten," I said, as blandly as I could.

"I'm going to prove it, and then I'm going to kill them both."

His name was Rackey, and though I knew he wasn't going to work as a bodyguard, I had an idea I might find a use later on for that barely contained violent impulse of his. "Listen, Mr. Rackey, it looks like the bodyguard position's already filled, but I have another proposition for you until a similar position opens up again. How would you like a job on the line at Collins aircraft?"

"I already been told they won't take me, on account of my dishonorable discharge."

"That's all right, pal." I sent him over to the plant with a strongly worded note of recommendation, complete with the suggestion that the order was coming from the old man himself. Whatever it was I figured Rackey could keep out of trouble on the floor until I figured out some better use for him.

The next candidate fit the bill better. Herman Park's history of violence was all within societally approved norms: the army (1931–37, 1942–46), Golden Gloves, and a stint with the Emporia Police Department in between. Somewhere along the line he'd had his nose broken, probably more than once.

"Why didn't you go back to Emporia after you mustered out?" I asked him.

"Wife moved down here for war work in '43. Wants me to get a job in an office or on an assembly line. I'd rather get my teeth pulled."

"How about the Wichita PD?"

"Not hiring. Too many ex-cops coming back, so many of them they're letting go some of the 4-Fs they hired during the fighting."

"Yeah, I heard about that. Some of those guys were walking around with a chip on their shoulder."

"Sure, everybody thought they were yellow. Tell you what, there were days in Germany I'd have traded places with any one of those guys, though."

I told Park he was hired and said I'd introduce him to Collins as soon as he was ready to carouse again.

"That's swell, Mr. Ogden."

I WAS FEELING like a good citizen, having found jobs for two returning vets, and I headed back to the plant to notify the personnel department, the head of which hated me. He had reason, since I regularly forced him to hire people he didn't want to on Everett Collins's say so. He was all right with Park, understanding as he did the need for a bodyguard for the boss, but he tried to put his foot down regarding Rackey.

"We've already got this Rackey fellow on file, and we're not hiring him." His reading glasses balanced on the tip of his nose, and on the word "not" he whipped them off for emphasis. He was right, of course; Rackey didn't meet any of the minimum requirements. Nonetheless I didn't like him telling me no.

"Mr. Whittaker, you will give Mr. Rackey a job. A job on the line. You will clear it with the shop steward, and if he has any trouble you report it directly to me. Is that understood?"

He picked up a manila file and waved it. "Do you know why he was thrown out of the Marines?"

"Don't care."

"He was court martialed and found guilty of cruelty to animals."

I thought he was kidding and started laughing.

"It's not funny. He killed a poodle that belonged to his colonel's wife."

"I don't believe you. There's no such charge in the Military Code of Justice."

"And when they arrested him for it they needed four MPs, two of whom were hospitalized with broken bones."

"You get all this from the Marines?" I asked, impressed with his thoroughness.

"You bet. We're still a military contractor, bub, and when I have to check someone's background I go to the source."

"Have him work on civilian planes, then," I said, and left him steaming.

I STOPPED IN at my own office and said hello to Mrs. Caspian, the secretary of the Publicity and Marketing Department. I liked her because she made no bones about not liking me. She knew enough about my real duties at Collins to hold me in contempt, and I admired her integrity in not pretending otherwise. She was a plump brunette who smelled of rosewater and Old Golds, and other than hating me she was an exemplary secretary. No one but Mrs. Caspian showed any resentment at working under a man who left the running of the department entirely to them and who took all the public credit for it. I didn't know beans about publicity, anyway, or about the airplane industry, either.

As a kid I was wild about airplanes, but I'd gotten over that well before the war, which had certainly drained whatever romance aviation had left for me. I might as well have been working for a company that manufactured washers or adding machines.

As long as I drew a paycheck and was allowed to come and go as I pleased I was fine. And make no mistake, I earned my living, wrangling our drunken founder in and out of roadhouses, hotels, and whorehouses.

On my desk were some roughs of trade magazine advertisements that I was meant to initial if they met my approval. This was a sham, since nine times out of ten I wouldn't show up at the office until long after deadline; oftentimes whoever placed it there would eventually recoup it and initial it himself. I scrawled my okay and dropped them on Mrs. Caspian's desk, and she ignored me. All was as it should be in the publicity and marketing department.

I STOPPED BY Collins's office to get a look at Millie Grau, on the pretense of checking to see if anything needed to be taken to the old man at home. There was nothing, Millie told me, then she asked me if I'd like a cup of coffee. "I don't usually brew any when Mr. Collins isn't in the office. He drinks it all day long. My gosh, I'd be all atwitter if I did that. But I sort of like a cup this time of the afternoon, if you know what I mean." I'd been drinking it all day at the diner, interviewing the bodyguards, but since it would involve her bending down to get the paper cups from the lower cabinet I told her yes.

She chirped about this and that as she busied herself with the coffee, and when she knelt down before the cabinet her black skirt pressed so tightly against her ass I thought I might pass out from the sudden rush of blood away from my head.

"I sure do miss having Mr. Collins around," she said. To my knowledge the old goat had never made any attempt to screw her; maybe it was her squeaking voice that short-circuited his normal urge to pursue anything in a skirt within groping distance, though I personally found that it added to her appeal. It wasn't out of any sense of professional decorum, either, since in addition to any number of girls on the production line, I knew Collins to have fucked a very homely predecessor of Millie's before the war, a certain Miss Schergren, enthusiastically and regularly. And a young woman with strong religious principles usually just excited his sense of sport; I'd chauffeured a Seventh Day Adventist up to Kansas City for a medical procedure just two weeks before I shipped off in '42.

I was standing close enough to her to smell the Doublemint on her breath—she must have been chewing it on the sly when I walked in—mingled with a tart scent redolent of citrus and cinnamon, a scent quickly overpowered by the percolating coffee.

"He should be himself in a day or two."

"No he won't," she said. "Have you ever had a broken rib? It hurts every time you breathe."

"Is that so?"

"And all they can do is wrap up your chest. It's awful."

"It must be."

"And you're such a good loyal friend to him."

I was paid to be, is what I thought, but I didn't want Miss Grau to think me cynical. "Well, he was my hero when I was a kid. All that Lucky Lindy-daring flyboy stuff. Goggles and rippling scarves and machine guns, shooting down German planes."

She giggled. "You sound like Donald."

"Who's Donald?"

She raised her left hand to display a decent sized rock, either a zircon or a pretty expensive piece of stone and silver. "Didn't you hear? I'm going to be Mrs. Donald Thorsten."

I certainly didn't want to marry Millie, and short of that I knew I'd never get the chance to take her to bed. Why, then, this ache upon hearing the news of her betrothal? "What's his line?"

"He's the new associate pastor at my church. Since last November."

"That's swell. I know you'll be happy."

"I'm so excited. The big day's this November, because Donald feels very strongly that a couple shouldn't marry if they haven't known one another at least a year."

"Wise man," I said.

She poured me a paper cupful of mild java, and I spent a few minutes extolling the virtues of married life before making myself scarce. It was close to the end of the shift and I didn't want to get stuck in the traffic heading westward away from the plant. There was no reason I couldn't have headed straight for home, but instead I headed for Red's.

RED'S WASN'T HOPPING. There was a copy of the *Evening Beacon* on the bar, and I was interested to see on page four that a man in his fifties had drunk himself to death in an apartment west of downtown, not far from the Masonic Home, while his wife rotted away in the next room, having died of undetermined causes several days earlier. The reporter, Fred Elting, was always a good one for nasty details on these sorts of stories, and he wasn't afraid to sensationalize. "What kind of city are we living in today, where a man is so afraid to report his wife's decease to the proper authorities that he pickles himself to death with gin while she molders by his side? Is this what our brave men fought for in Europe and Asia?"

To tell you the truth, Fred, I wasn't giving Wichita and its lonesome drunks much thought when I was over there.

There wasn't much else of interest in the paper, and I fell into talking to one of the b-girls. Her name was Barbara, and she looked like she must have been a lot of fun before the war. The 1946 model had a drinker's puffy face, though, and a little bit of a paunch that her girdle wasn't quite containing beneath her dress. "That's a pretty thin dress for March," I said.

"It's been pretty balmy the last few days," she said, crossing her legs, the slit in her dress aligning to give me a perfect view of the top of her right stocking. Her legs were okay, and the leer she was giving me suggested that a few good times might still be had with the old girl. "Where's your friend?"

"He got into a fight the other night," I said, thinking she meant Collins. "His bodyguard let him get his ribs broken."

"Wait a minute, the bodyguard has a bodyguard?"

Was she really that drunk or that stupid? "You're talking about Billy Clark?"

"Good-looking fella sits in a booth and watches you and old Collins drinking and having fun?"

"That's him."

"I always feel kind of sorry for him."

"He got beaten up too, and he lost his job on top of it, so your pity's not entirely misplaced."

"Gosh. Lost his job and everything?"

"He's a goddamn idiot. What kind of numbskull bodyguard starts a fight with a couple of big hayseeds he couldn't whip sober?"

"Well, that Collins is a creep and a pervert."

I had no argument against that. "He pays okay," I countered.

"He was screwing my girlfriend Lottie, had her on all fours. Pushed her face down onto the mattress, just spit in his hand and did it pretty as you please. Boy she was mad. Threatened to go to the cops and report him as a pervert."

"Cops don't care."

"Sure they do! It's called sodomy and there's a law against it in the state of Kansas."

"I mean the cops don't care about it when Everett Collins does it."

"Well he sure seemed scared because when he sobered up he paid her two hundred and fifty dollars afterward not to squawk."

All this sex talk, on top of my earlier encounter with Millie Grau, was getting me thinking I needed my ashes hauled one way or another tonight. I thought of my beautiful wife at home, and comparing her in my head with the alcoholic harridan before me there was no way to find her wanting. But Barbara wasn't going to ruin it by talking afterward about baby clothes or what religion to raise the little interloper in.

Fifteen minutes later I was tucking my shirt back into my pants while she tugged her threadbare rayon panties back on, then deftly rehooked her brassiere behind her back. Her armpits were stubbly and dusted with something like talcum.

"In Europe the girls don't shave under their arms," I said, rolling the window down to toss the used rubber out onto the gravel.

"That's disgusting." She seemed genuinely offended.

"You get used to it. When I first got back my wife's shaved pits looked odd to me."

She got quiet for a minute while she pulled her stockings on and attached the garters. "I don't sleep with married men as a rule," she said, finally and with undisguised peevishness.

I bristled at the implied slur on my character. In a spiteful moment I pulled a ten from my wallet and put it in her cold, sweaty little hand. "Just a little something to get you by."

She looked at it for a second like it was a turd some little song-bird had laid on her palm, then wadded it up and stuck it in my shirt pocket. "What the hell do you take me for?" she said. "I don't take money for screwing."

"Sorry," I said, unable to suppress a grin. When we were fully dressed I followed her back inside and bought her a drink.

"Here's to you," she said, raising her glass.

"*Post coitum animal triste,* as my grandpa used to say." Down the hatch, burning all the way.

"What's that mean? That a toast?"

"Means I ought to think about getting home for dinner."

"When you coming back next?" she asked.

I didn't answer, just got up off of the stool and walked away. The bartender on duty, a lanky, hollow-cheeked fellow, watched me go with a look on his face like I'd just shot his mother, and I realized the truth of the old saw that there's someone for everyone in this world.

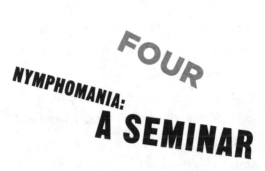

FOUR
NYMPHOMANIA:
A SEMINAR

ANOTHER ENVELOPE HAD arrived at work from my secret admirer in Salem, Massachusetts, this one addressed to WAYNE ODGON COLLINS AIR WITCHIT KANS. I halfway wondered whether he wasn't having fun with the spelling of my name on purpose. This time the note inside read:

YOU KILLED HER AND YOUR GOING TO PAY
THE PRICE

That evening at home I scanned both afternoon papers. The top of the news on KFH was a stickup at a local restaurant that had happened too late for the papers. The cook was dead and so was the stickup man, shot by the cops, and the news man took pains to point out the fact that the robber was a returning vet. It didn't mention whether he'd been able to find a job since he got back, or whether his wife had been fucking around in his absence, or whether he'd seen combat.

The crime reporter told the story in a high-pitched nasal voice that was nearly as grating as the sound of the donnybrook the Dunphys' were having downstairs. I was in my easy chair in the parlor, as close to the radio as possible, weighing the relative merits of going out on the town versus staying in and reading. I was midway through a book from the twenties entitled *Sexual History of the World War*, a pretty good read that Sally didn't want in the house. "What if someone comes over and sees it on the shelf?" she'd said when I brought it home from the secondhand book store. It was a pretty good read. I had an idea that America's sexual habits must have changed some after the boys came back from Europe in 1918, having learned about cuntlapping and blowjobs and various other bits of European business, and similarly in the last few years I'd seen many an Iowa farm boy wake up to the myriad possibilities inherent in human coition. I wanted badly to finish the chapter on the Regulation of Army Brothels, but the Dunphys' clashes had been running long and loud of late, and I decided to join Herman Park and the boss on their nocturnal rounds.

There was a downside to this, too; the old man was in fine form since the end of his convalescence, nastier than usual and quicker to anger. Those periods of jolly drunkenness between short-tempered hangover and havoc-wreaking, pie-eyed inebriation were shorter and rarer than before.

I caught up with them as we'd tentatively planned at a blind pig above an old carriage house at 12th and Bitting in Riverside. The proprietor was an old friend of mine, a luckless boozer abandoned years ago by a wife he never stopped thinking or talking about. He and Collins were getting along like a house afire when I arrived, and Park was sitting in a chair drinking a ginger ale.

"Keep trying to tell this sumbitch he needs a goddamn drink," Collins said when I walked in.

"I'm driving you around, Mr. Collins, I like to be alert," Park said.

"I'll have a bourbon, neat," I said to my old pal Norman. He grinned, the gin blossoms on his nose and cheeks a deeper red than usual.

Collins was in one of his professorial moods, and I had apparently interrupted a long discourse on the comparative sexual needs of men and women, which he now resumed.

"On the other hand, though," Collins said, "we have the women who can't settle for one man. These are a rare breed. Most become prostitutes. Others bring shame upon good families by making spectacles of themselves. When I was coming up in Michigan there was a woman in our town, the wife of a judge, no less, who was discovered to have taken on no fewer than five lovers over a period of fifteen years. Now she was a handsome woman, but what sort of wife isn't satisfied with a judge? And we knew, we men of the town, that the judge was perfectly capable in bed because he himself was known to keep mistresses. Now not everyone admired him for it, but it was proof that he could satisfy a woman, and by extension proof that his wife was insane. The scientific term is nymphomaniac."

NORMAN SHOOK HIS head and looked at the floor. Park sat back in his chair and drank his ginger ale while Collins went on for a while in this vein: the horrors of menstruation, women's hormones leading eventually, inevitably, to insanity of one kind or another.

As always Norman's face hair was unwashed and a little too long, his glasses badly smudged, and he looked like he'd rather not listen any more. "Let's go meet some women," I said.

Park was already out of his chair. "I know a roadhouse way out on Tyler Road has some pretty wild ones," he said.

"Guess we might as well before I get much drunker," the boss said. I paid our bill (I was reimbursed every two weeks for expenses, since Collins wasn't to be trusted with great amounts of cash on these expeditions), and we took our leave. At the bottom of the rickety staircase that led downstairs the old man stumbled and fell forward, hitting the door. A stream of obscenities and animal howls erupted, and when Park tried to reach for him Collins swung a wild fist in his direction.

"Goddamn broken ribs, Jesus Christ, I need back on the fucking morphine. Ogden, you get on that first thing in the goddamn morning." His voice broke on that second "goddamn."

THE ROADHOUSE PARK took us to was indeed full of wild women, and the boss's mood cleared right up on arrival. He was talking to a pretty brunette who was dressed for a much better class of place than this, and she was rubbing his sleeve and laughing with delight at whatever he was saying to her, probably an indecent proposition. Park and I had earned our keep for the night.

Park stood in the doorway beckoning me. "There's a dark Plymouth been following us since the blind pig; I don't know if they were on our tail before or not, but that's my guess. Parked in the back corner of the lot, guy's sitting behind the wheel still."

I went through the back door and moved to the parking lot, lurking among the twenty or so cars until I spotted the Plymouth and its driver, watching the front door of the roadhouse with a camera perched on top of the dash, a new-looking Speed Graphic. It was Hiram Fish, whom Mrs. Collins occasionally entrusted with the job of following her husband around gathering evidence of his misdeeds. There wasn't much point to it besides masochism that I could see; devout Catholic that she was, she wouldn't be able to use the photos in a divorce case.

On one occasion during the war, the old bitch had shown the old man a set of photos and demanded an explanation. They showed him at a party in the company of a homely and heavily made-up woman wearing only panties, garter belt, and black stockings, a getup similar to which most of the women in the background were also wearing. The men were in shirtsleeves and most wore paper hats marked with stars and stripes. He explained to the Mrs. that this was a birthday party for Uncle Sam, and that as defense contractors he and some of his colleagues were required to attend. When he added that the girl with him was a good patriotic American girl whose contribution to the war effort was made horizontally, Mrs. Collins slapped him. He backhanded her in response, knocking her into a cabinet filled with little porcelain figures, some of which fell off their shelves. She started crying, picking up the shards of the precious little things, and he left the house looking for a fight or a fuck or both. Or at least that's the way Collins told me the story; I was in Italy at the time, or maybe still in England, fighting the Nazi menace in my own round-about fashion.

In any event, Fish represented a threat to my status quo, and I didn't like the looks of him anyway, with his little pencil moustache like a slick villain in a movie and his too-perfectly brilliantined hair. Not to mention there was always something a little shady about these ex-cops who take up snooping, just one step removed from window peepers and dickflashers, as far as I was concerned. I retraced my steps and went all the way around the building, then crept, doubled over, to Collins's Packard. I opened up the right rear door and grabbed the baseball bat I kept stashed under the front seat.

Then I rose to my full height and strode across the gravel to Fish's Plymouth. He tried frantically to start it up, but before he got it into gear I'd already smashed the windshield, spiderwebbing the glass badly enough to prevent its operation until the shards were busted out. Fish scrambled out the driver's door.

"You crazy son of a bitch, what the hell you mean busting my windshield?"

I swung again, left-handed this time, and caught him in the shin. He went down in hysterics and I got him a good one on the forearm. I could hear bone cracking, and I figured he was probably out of commission for the evening.

A crowd had formed at the door of the roadhouse. Park was walking towards me, saying something conciliatory to a concerned stranger who was wondering whether I needed bringing to heel. I reached into the front seat and grabbed Fish's Speed Graphic, took out the film holder and pulled the sheet out of it, then opened half a dozen more he had laying on the seat. I didn't know if they contained latent images of Collins or not; I scattered the raw negatives onto the gravel. Then I set the camera on top of the Plymouth's hood and clipped it like Ted Goddamn Williams. It flew a good twenty feet and banged into a Studebaker.

"Mr. Ogden," Park was saying.

"Yeah."

"Are you listening? This is important."

"Yeah."

"Mr. Ogden, I'm the bodyguard. It makes me look bad when you take it upon yourself to do something like this. I'm still new, I know, but next time just tell me what to do and I'll do it."

"You're a good man, Park. Let's have a drink." I was well pleased at having hired him. We walked back inside and found the old man ensconced in a booth with his brunette, rubbing the inside of her thigh, completely unaware of the activity outside.

I GOT HOME exhausted at two in the morning and was relieved to find the lights out in the apartment. I undressed and got into bed and closed my eyes, and just as I began to relax into a state conducive to sleep the lamp came on.

"You son of a bitch," she said, up on one elbow. Then she wheeled around and got out of bed, looking like she might hit me.

I was in worse trouble than I'd first assumed. "What the hell?" I said.

"If you won't tell me what's wrong I can't fix it."

Despite herself she was starting to cry. I was in bad trouble, I knew it; she hadn't ever cried in my presence beyond her eyes getting a little wet, not even on the occasion of her mother's death.

She struggled to get control and spoke again. "You don't love me any more."

Jumping Jesus, what do you say to that? "Course I do, baby, what are you talking about?"

She swallowed. She was regaining some of her control. "You're out and about almost every night, I eat dinner with your mother more often than with you, ever since I told you about the baby you've barely touched me. You like that boss of yours more than me."

I laughed at that, and she gave me a look of pure snake venom. Beautiful and feminine as she was, she was a big girl nonetheless, and she'd hit me before, and hard. "Baby, that couldn't be further from the truth. I can't stand the son of a bitch."

"Then why are you out with him every night?"

"Because since I got back, that's what my job is. Babysitter. Didn't you ever wonder why the head of the Publicity and Marketing Department doesn't go in to work most days until ten in the morning? My job is to keep a muzzle on the old man, and the only public relations I do is keeping the old pervert out of the *Beacon* and the *Eagle*."

She wiped both cheeks with the heels of her palms. "You aren't seeing somebody else?"

"Hell, no, why would I? I got the sweetest piece of tail in the state right here at home." Despite herself I had made her giggle. "If you doubt me you can come along some night and watch me and the bodyguard sitting around watching the boss carouse." In fact Collins would love that; he'd probably make a pass at her, pregnant or not.

"If you're not seeing somebody else how come we're down to four or five times a week any more?"

"Every night's a tall order, baby. I'm thirty-one years old, and coming home late the way I do . . . half the time you're asleep anyway."

"I'm not asleep right now," she said with the suggestion of a smile, lifting her nightie and exposing that exceptionally lovely torso. I stared at her body, her pubic hair especially black against her slightly swollen winter-white belly, nipples wide and erect, and said a little prayer of thanks for this heaven-sent carnal bounty.

Doctor Ezra Groff kept a little house just west of Hillside he'd reconfigured as a doctor's office, with two examining rooms and a little surgery in the back. For a long time he'd been the town's most reliable angelmaker, but toward the end of the thirties there was a local crackdown and he started referring girls in trouble to out-of-town docs like Beck in Kansas City. Enough girls of prominent birth had been helped out of sticky situations that he avoided prosecution, and his practice had survived, though it couldn't be said to have thrived. I was the only patient in the waiting room at ten in the morning.

His elderly nurse Lois had me fill out some paperwork, since I hadn't been in since '41. Her bright red hair had gone pinkish and she'd put on a good deal of weight, which may have accounted for the slight limp she'd taken on since I saw her last. She chatted amiably while I wrote, talked about what a precocious little boy I'd been, insisting on knowing the Latin names for treatments and ailments and body parts when I was as young as five. I liked Lois. According to my father, she'd been Dr. Groff's girlfriend as well as his nurse in the old days, long before Dr. Groff's wife was carted off to the state lunatic asylum at Larned. I wondered if they were still at it.

In the examination room I sat on the table with my shirt needlessly off on nurse Lois's instructions. The whole place smelled like mercurochrome and ammonia and mold.

"Well, young Ogden," Groff said when he came in, stubbing a dead butt into the ashtray. "Back from the war, I see."

"Back since spring," I said.

"And what's troubling you that the VA can't fix for free?"

"It's for a friend."

He snorted. "It always is. This friend, what's her name?"

"What the hell, this was one old man who knew how to keep a secret. Everett Collins."

Groff's wild grey eyebrows lifted, and I couldn't tell whether he was dubious or impressed. "Go on."

"He broke a rib or two, got sucker-punched by a big farm boy in a road house."

"Painful, broken ribs. Awful bad."

"That's the thing. He wants to know if I can't get him a prescription for some morphine."

"I want to make sure I understand. This is the same Everett Collins that founded Collins Aircraft?"

"The same. I'm working for him."

"All right. You don't want morphine, it's too hard to administer properly. I've got something new, just as good and not as addictive."

"The prescription needs to be in my name, for discretion's sake."

He nodded, eyes closed. His eyelids were veined and purplish. "Of course." He grabbed a pad and started writing. "It's called Hycodan, what we call a semi-synthetic opioid. Cross between codeine and thebaine, if that means anything to you."

"Thanks, Dr. Groff."

"Your mother was in for woman trouble a couple of weeks ago. She says your wife is expecting."

I winced. I didn't want to hear about my mother or any kind of woman trouble she might be having. I didn't want to think about the pregnancy, either, for that matter. "That's right."

"Hope it doesn't ruin that pretty figure of hers. She's quite a gal."

I smiled, or tried to. "Sure is."

"How's she taking her new condition?"

"How do you mean?"

"Moods. Morning sickness. All that."

"She's taken to crying. She never used to do that. She's quicker to anger."

"Get used to it. A baby in the womb sets off a whole string of chemical and hormonal reactions in a woman's body that you and I can be thankful we'll never have to deal with." He started scribbling on a pad of paper. "Now, you might mention to Mr. Collins that I'm angling for the position of County Coroner next year."

"I'll do that."

"I'm not asking for a quid pro quo. You know that. All I'm saying is I wouldn't mind having some powerful people in my corner when the time comes."

I took the prescription from his hand. "I don't think he'll forget this."

THE PHARMACIST ON Hillside across from Wesley hospital filled the scrip without comment or question. "Take that up to Mrs. Perkey at the cash register and she'll ring you up."

Mrs. Perkey beamed as she took the prescription from me and rang it up. "Wayne Ogden, isn't it nice seeing you."

"Nice to see you, too, Mrs. Perkey," I said, only vaguely aware of ever having known her and grateful to the pharmacist for having supplied the name.

"Your mother and I were just talking about your blessed event."

"She's beside herself," I said, though this was just a guess. I hadn't seen or spoken to the old bird since I found out about it. I guessed Sally must have told her. "She's got step-grandchildren, but this is the first of her own."

I paid her and walked out. "Hope you get to feeling better right quick," she called after me.

THE BOSS GLOWERED at me when I walked into his office, his shoulders hunched and hangover tense, a condition that had to exacerbate the pain in his ribcage. Before he had a chance to snap at me I dropped the bag with the Hycodan on the blotter that sat atop his massive mahogany desk. "Instructions are written on the side of the bag."

It was as though a state of grace washed over him just then. His musculature relaxed visibly, and he exhaled as though he'd been holding it in all morning. His torn ear got redder, his eyes brightened and he opened the bag like a little kid digging into his Christmas stocking. "Morphine. Hot diggetty."

"Isn't morphine. Something new. Better than morphine."

"The hell you say."

"Fix you right up, is what the doc says."

Without reading the directions he unscrewed the bottle top and tossed one into his mouth and crunched it. On the desk was an elaborately detailed model of the Collins L-120, the biplane that had put the company on the map in the twenties. Lindbergh flew one of the first, and later Wiley Post and Amelia Earhart did too. I nearly bought a used one in the days after I finished college and before I got my first job at Collins, even though I didn't have an aviator's license. These days I couldn't have been more indifferent to the whole business of flying, but the sight of the dark blue fuselage and the robin's-egg blue wings by the light of Collins's desk lamp brought forth a little twinge of innocent nostalgia. I almost wished I could make myself care about the damned things again.

"The old fishcunt was pretty sore at me this morning, Ogden," he said with a grin.

"How's that?"

"Mr. Fish is dunning her for his medical bills. She says I ought to pay them. I told her I didn't know what the hell she was talking about."

"She ought to hire somebody better than that to follow you around."

"I think she just likes that pretty moustache of his. Always talking about how handsome this movie star or that one is. Occurs to me you should have messed up his face, maybe. Thinking maybe if he wasn't so pretty she'd quit hiring him."

"Problem with that is she might stumble onto someone halfway competent, then you'd be screwed."

"That might be right. Anyhow, I think she might be in cahoots with some of the board. There's a move afoot to fire you, boy, you know that?"

"I didn't."

"You and me both. One or two of 'em on the board want to replace me with the wife, can you beat that?"

"Doesn't seem likely."

"They think I'm irresponsible. Want her sitting in here doing what they tell her to do. Because her last name's Collins. Inspires confidence. Look like I'd just stepped aside for her."

This was bad news. I might not stay at Collins forever, but if I did go I was determined to leave at a time of my choosing and on my own terms. Another goddamn mess for me to fix, and probably without much in the way of help from Uncle Blackout here. "Who's with her?"

"Huff, that sanctimonious son of a bitch." Ernest Huff, the comp-troller, was a notorious straight arrow, stickler for detail and all-around pain in the dick. "Latham, probably, he doesn't like the way I do things. I'll ask a couple of the fellows who else there is, and when I find out we'll fix the sons of bitches." He swished some saliva around in his mouth to get rid of the chunks of pill. "Get me a drink of water."

I left the room and stepped out into the reception area, where I was rewarded with a sweet look from Millie Grau. I poured a glass of water from the cooler and went back into the office, where Collins swigged half of it down and gargled.

"You shouldn't drink water," he said after he swallowed the rest. "Know why?"

"No. Why?"

"Fish fuck in it."

FIVE

THE BEST JOB

I EVER HAD

WAS TRYING TO find an excuse to get back up to see Vickie in Kansas City but was stymied by the boss's baffling failure to knock up any more wayward girls. She sent me a letter at work—the only address I'd provided her—promising me a hell of a good time when I got there. I answered with a non-committal post card. I needed to get back to KC. It wasn't just Vickie; I was looking into a potential source of income separate from the job.

The idea had come to me when I passed a cigar store that my grand-father used to frequent on his occasional trips to visit us in Wichita. Trebegs were his brand, and he used to send me off with a two-dollar bill to buy a boxful and let me keep the change. Another popular item at the cigar store were dirty comic books and postcards, kept under the counter and only available to customers the clerk knew well. Good old Grandpa bought me a stack of Tijuana Bibles when I was twelve, a real godsend for my budding career as a chronic onanist, which lasted until I was fifteen and started getting laid regularly.

The severe, lipless relic manning the counter in the present day had stared at me as though offended by my very existence; he certainly lacked the hail-fellow-well-met demeanor that any sort of under-the-counter trade demands of a merchant, so I didn't bother inquiring. Something came to me as I walked out the door, though, the memory of a wholesaler that used to provide me with pornographic photos in Rome: the Nonpareil Photographic Studio of Kansas City, Missouri.

One night Park and I were along for the ride with Collins at a blind pig up near Newton that one of his high-rolling buddies had told him about. It was in a big farmhouse in a neighborhood on the outskirts of town, and it was better appointed than a lot of real bars I'd been in. The boss was in an expansive mood, after a long and friendly conversation with the proprietor regarding the ins and outs of rural lawbreaking. They established at length that bringing whores into the blind pig, even just for tonight, might jeopardize the barkeep's delicate position with local law enforcement. It was decided that after a couple more drinks we would head for the Crosley Hotel just north of downtown and find some there.

Collins stood with his arm on the mantle above the fireplace and smirked. "Admit it, boys, this is the best goddamn job you ever had."

Park nodded and I just smiled. Sure, it wasn't exactly coal mining, and I was grateful to have a position that got me out of the house—when I'd left that evening, Sally was listening to "Baby Snooks" on KFH, and if I'd had to listen to a whole half hour of that shit I'd have blown my brains out—but this wasn't the best job I ever had, not by a mile.

In the army I used to look back at my pre-war self with a mixture of nostalgia and pity. What the hell had I thought I was accomplishing selling airplanes? The QM Corps gave me thrilling and lucrative work. Men needed the things I offered for sale. Women, some of them beautiful women, relied on me for protection and income, and the army relied on me to distribute whatever I wasn't able to reroute and sell elsewhere. It was a good life, and by the time it came to its violent end I could see my sweet situation beginning to unravel. There would be no place for me in Italy after the war, without the army to protect my position and provide my clientele, and my stab wound—for which I managed to con my way into a Purple Heart—got me home months earlier than was right.

So acting as bag man and babysitter for an alcoholic skirtchaser came in a poor second. Hell, I had a job as a kid selling pots and pans door to door that might give this one a run for its money.

THE FRONT DESK man at the Crosley greeted Collins by name and told him to go right up. "Elevator's broken, you'll have to use the stairs."

The stairs smelled like a lioness in heat had pissed her way up to the fourth floor, by which time Collins was gasping. "What the hell happened to this place?" I asked. "This used to be a nice hotel."

"Whores and hopheads now," Collins said between wheezes. He knocked on the door of room 406, which was answered by a tired looking forty-year-old with blonde bangs wearing a tattered silk robe that hung open, revealing a matching set of underwear underneath.

"Benny called and said you was coming up, but he didn't say you brought friends. Let me call a couple girls and we'll all of us have a party." The circles under her eyes were dark as bruises, and I suspected that once she doffed that robe we'd be treated to the sight of track marks inside her elbows.

"I think I'm going to make an early night of it, boss."

"What the hell?" the old man said, his fury manifesting itself instantly and, as usual, without warning. That chopped-up ear was the color of a July tomato. "I'm paying, where the hell do you get off saying no to a free piece of ass?"

"Hey, fellahs, not in the hallway, please," the girl said, trying to usher us into the room. "There's still citizens live in this hotel."

"I'll get a cab," I said, and headed for the stairs.

"How about you?" he asked Park. "You a fucking water lily too?"

"I'll have me a piece, sure."

"Good. Go on get in there. Ogden, you're fired, you lousy little queer piece of shit."

Without turning around I waved them goodnight. This wasn't the first time he'd fired me in such a state, and in the morning he'd be lucky if he remembered enough to regret it. Everett Collins didn't know it, but he'd just sent me on a much-needed vacation.

I HAILED A cab on North Main and told him to drive out toward Red's. I shouldn't have gotten to thinking about Italy, where I was my own boss, even if several thousand men could legitimately claim to have the power to give me orders. I pulled from the inside pocket of my sport coat a letter I'd been carrying for two weeks, from my old buddy Lester, stationed now in occupied Japan. After the usual pleasantries and perfunctory asking after my family, he got to the real gist of the matter:

*You ought to be here, Oggie, there is action all the time
and guys arriving looking for a game or a girl or a fix and
man oh man its wide open. Local enforcers are all on the
run and that's the way it is going to go around here till they
get thereselves ready to re-join civization. Come on back to
Mother Army, Oggy, all is forgiven. If you re-up there is
strings can be puled and you will end up here and not Europe
where the game is already winding down.*

Red's was no busier than I'd have expected on a Tuesday. My
b-girl Barbara was sitting with the off-duty bartender who'd given me
the dirty look before, and she made a point of looking away from me
when I passed by. I was almost glad for her, and it simplified things
around Red's if she wasn't looking for another turn.

I didn't see any other girls that appealed, though. I hurried through
a whisky soda and stepped outside into the night air, warm and still for
a Kansas March. I was on the verge of going inside to phone for a cab
when I saw what looked like an old friend sitting in the far corner of
the lot. It was a 1916 Hudson, a Phaeton Super 6, identical to the one
I'd owned as a boy, painted white or something near it. Someone had
taken good care of it; it gleamed in the moonlight, and I wanted to hear
if it ran as nice as it looked.

Before I'd considered what I was doing I found myself climbing in
and fooling with the starter, and then I was driving eastward toward
town. The Super 6 ran as well as mine ever had, and I wished I could
congratulate the owner; maybe someday I would; maybe I'd even let
on that I was the one who'd stolen it that beautiful spring night back
in March of '46.

What the hell, I was going to Kansas City to get my ashes hauled and to talk to the owner of the Nonpareil Photographic Studio. Lester could probably use the connection even if I couldn't.

I tried not to wake Sally as I rummaged the bedroom closet in the dark, but she wasn't sleeping well. "You're packing a bag?"

"Ssshh. Go back to sleep. Business trip. Five-fifteen train."

"You never said anything about a business trip."

I buckled the suitcase shut and gave her a peck on her cheek, cupping her left breast as I did so. She smelled like soap and cigarettes, and for just a second I loved her as much as I ever had.

By THE TIME I abandoned the Super 6 in the parking lot of Union Station, it had started to get cool. Inside I waited in line behind a stout lady in a mink coat topped with a fox stole. The fox's glass eyes were both loose and hanging from its furry face by what seemed to be strips of rotten suede, and he stared wall-eyed at the early morning crowd while his mistress sorted through some sort of complicated ticketing problem with the clerk. I wasn't paying any attention to the details, since I was in no particular hurry; I had a good hour and a half before my train left. I was enjoying the subtle, almost musical interplay of her bullying whine and the clerk's stubborn, irritated monotone. At length, another ticket window opened and I moved over to it. By the time I'd transacted my business the confrontation at the other window had degenerated into shouting, and my ticketseller glanced over and snickered. The fat lady had been joined by an expensively dressed middle-aged man the size of a twelve-year-old, and he stood behind the lady as if for protection.

"Looks like Casper Milquetoast from the funny pages, don't he?" the ticketseller said, and I had to laugh. The little fellow did, right down to his rimless spectacles.

I bought the early editions of the *Morning Beacon* and the *Morning Eagle* from the midget who ran the newsstand and took a seat in the Harvey House. The Harvey girl who took my order looked like she'd rather be sleeping, and I asked if I should buy her a cup of coffee too. She faked a chuckle, stifled a yawn, and explained that this wasn't a normal waking hour for her, that she was covering a shift for a girl whose mother was ill. "Normally I don't get up until seven at least. Boy, I don't know how people do it. I'm so cranky I gotta watch I don't slap somebody."

By THE TIME the Harvey girl brought my bacon and eggs I was almost done with the *Eagle*. It seemed odd, the idea that there was still news to report after the war was won. But people were still robbing grocery stores and crashing their cars and having Chamber of Commerce meetings, still drowning and going on strike and breaking jail. The funnies, on the other hand, weren't as funny as they used to be. What ever happened to *Thimble Theater*? Was *Krazy Kat* in the paper any more? *Mutt and Jeff* were still in the *Beacon*, I was relieved to note, but they weren't as funny and mean as they used to be, just a couple of shitkickers telling corny jokes. And if Casper Milquetoast was in print I hadn't seen him.

I went back to the newsstand after breakfast and bought a couple of magazines for the trip. The rocking motion of the train might lull me to sleep, but at that moment I felt excited enough that I imagined I'd stay awake the whole trip, and I didn't want to be bored.

It was still dark when the train pulled out of the station, and I unfurled my copy of *Life*. Like a comet shooting through the sky announcing an auspicious event, the page I happened to open to had a photo essay on the establishment of a permanent military base in Japan. I started reading the article, but before I was done with it my late night caught up with me and I was out.

When I awoke it was light and there was a stocky man of eighty or more sitting across from me. A farmer, I guessed, shrunken a bit from his days of physical labor but not gone entirely to seed. "Morning," he said.

"Morning," I said, looking out the window and trying to figure out where we were.

"Where you headed? Chicago?" He had on a suit that looked like one my grandfather used to wear, the height of fashion thirty years before. His shirt collar came halfway up his throat.

"Kansas City," I said.

"Me, I'm headed for Chicago. Going to be married to a woman I've been corresponding with."

"That's good," I said, though I suspected it wasn't.

"Want to see her picture?" Without waiting for my reply he pulled a glossy four-by-five print from his coat pocket and handed it over. The woman in the picture was no older than forty and generously daubed with kohl and rouge like Theda Bara from the silent pictures, though the dress she wore was of more recent vintage. Her broad smile, more of a leer, really, showed an irregular mouthful of jagged teeth. "Ain't she something?"

"She is. Known her long?"

"Since't last September."

"Ever met her in the flesh?"

"No, sir, this here'll be the first time."

"That's terrific."

"She's going to come back and live on the farm with me. She's tired of city ways, she says."

I took a closer look at the old gent. His suit was out of date, but it had been a good one when it was made, and a heavy gold chain hung from his coat. "Say, you don't know the time, do you? My watch stopped."

He reached for that chain and, as I expected, out came a solid gold watch bigger than a silver dollar. "Nine twenty, just about."

"Thanks. So how'd you get in touch with this gal?"

"One of them lonely hearts correspondence clubs. We had a whole mess of interests in common. Gin rummy, for a start. Stamps, for another."

"I used to collect stamps," I said.

"It's a wholesome hobby. I also breed horses, Morgans, and turns out she's loved horses her whole life and hasn't had a chance to be around 'em."

"Good for her," I said, feeling a little sorry for the horny old bastard across from me.

"Course my daughters and sons-in-laws are dead set against it. Afraid I'll leave the farm and the money to her and not them. Well, sir, if they don't treat her like a mother, then that's just what'll happen."

I gathered that part of his desire to remarry was the idea that he'd missed out on something the first time around. "Fern was a mean woman, and her daughters are all three mean and crabbed as she was. I'll tell you something on the QT. I was married to that woman thirty-seven miserable years, and she only let me make a woman out of her eight times, and the last three of those was by force. I didn't care no more about it, I was done with her. When she hanged herself, you know what I said? Good."

He leaned forward, the multitude of tracks outside signaling our imminent arrival at KC's Union Station.

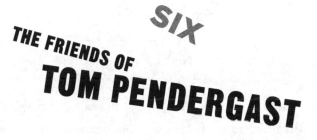

SIX
THE FRIENDS OF
TOM PENDERGAST

S INCE THE VISIT was a surprise anyway I decided to grab a taxi and go straight to Vickie's place in Westport. It was a hell of a lot colder than it had been in Wichita, and the cabbie laughed when I mentioned it. "Yeah, yesterday fooled you. You thought it was really springtime, didn't you? Big arctic front coming down from Canada. Snowing in Chicago right now, is what it says on the radio."

"You don't say."

"Could have some here tonight. And yesterday it got up into the high sixties."

He was about my age and looked to be in sound health. "Let me ask you something, buddy. You in the war?"

"Sure was," he said. "You?"

"Yeah. Miss it?"

He looked at me in the rear view mirror like I was either kidding or crazy. "Hell, no. I never had a worse time in my damn life than in the lousy goddamn Navy. There's a petty officer I came damn close to killing. If I thought there was any chance of getting away with a murder on a United States aircraft carrier I by God would have done it, too, no regrets."

I almost laughed; there was the Navy for you. An Army man would have figured out a way, and a Marine would have just killed the son of a bitch and damn the consequences.

IT HADN'T OCCURRED to me in the slightest that Vickie might be less than thrilled to find me standing there all chipper and horny on her welcome mat.

"Jesus, Wayne, don't you ever send a telegram or anything?" She looked worse than I'd ever seen her look, which was still a cut above most women. Puffy-eyed, her hair a wreck, no makeup, and wearing just a tattered bathrobe, she gave me an up and down that, while still disapproving, was moving into the realm of the friendly. "You know perfectly goddamn well I work nights."

"I could use some shuteye myself," I said. "I only slept an hour or two on the train."

"No, huh-uh. I need to sleep, and I mean sleep and nothing else."

"How about I crash on the couch?"

"Nuh-uh. You be on your way. You're lucky 'cause I'm off tonight, but right now I'm going to sleep. Come back at four or five and you can take me out on a proper date and then maybe we'll see what happens."

When she shut the door on me she had a look on her face that was almost affectionate.

FIFTEEN MINUTES LATER a cab was dropping me off outside a dingy office building on Troost. The building directory led me to a suite on the top floor, and when I rang the buzzer no one answered at first. After a third and a fourth buzz, a baldheaded man with a painfully annoyed look on his face answered.

"Whatever it is I don't need it. Scram," he said. He was in his shirt-sleeves and his suspenders were frayed. One lens of his black-framed eyeglasses was cracked.

"Hold on," I said, and stuck my foot in the door.

"Scram," he said again.

"Used to be a customer. United States Army Quartermaster Corps in Rome. Wayne Ogden's the name, if that means anything to you."

He cocked his head. "Ogden. The hell you say. I'm Merle Tessler."

"I used to order quite a lot of material from you. I was in town, thought I'd look you up."

"Huh," he said. "Never ever had a customer visit in the flesh before."

"Glad to see you're still in business. I have a buddy stationed in Japan right now, running the same type operation I used to. Thought maybe you could send him a set on approval."

"Hell, come on in. We could sure set something up like that."

IT WAS LIKE any other photographic studio, with a skylight above and a portrait lighting kit. A corner of the room was used as a set, with various pieces of furniture. There was a darkroom in the corner, and a number of cameras in different formats, including one I hadn't expected to see.

"Is that a Bolex, there? Swiss?"

"You know your gear, don't you?"

"My grandfather was a photographer, and my dad was an amateur. So you're making movies."

"Yep. Sixteen millimeter. Started making stags right about six months back."

"No fooling. I bet my buddy in Japan would like to get his hands on some of those."

From a file cabinet he extracted a folder and handed it to me. Inside were pictures of girls, most of them better-than-average looking, getting fucked by an assortment of disreputable-looking men. Most of the men had the haggard, hopeless look of dope fiends, skinny degenerates with well-defined ribcages and jutting Adam's apples.

"That's the regular sex stuff. Shot those last month."

"I don't recognize any of the girls from the sets I was selling."

"No, the turnover's pretty high. Plus which the customers like to see new girls every once in a while." He handed me another folder. In this one, girls in lingerie and black stockings abused one another. One of them showed a blonde in a girdle using a cat-o'-nine-tails to torment a sallow brunette tied face-forward to a painter's ladder. The brunette was no actress, the expression of horror on her face laughably false. "These here are real popular too."

"I know the genre. I remember one, had a gal in a French maid's costume with a feather duster sticking out her ass."

Tessler laughed fondly at the memory. "You never ought to have gotten the likes of that one. That was made to order for a customer in Marshall, Minnesota. Model was a hillbilly gal from Tennessee someplace, damned if I can remember her name. One of those who'd do just about anything, I used her when I got special requests. Stuff the other gals wouldn't."

"Like what?"

He reached into his file cabinet and pulled out a third folder, marked "MADE-To-OrdEr," and handed it to me with an odd, crooked half-grin. Inside was a passport to a whole wide wonderful world of idiosyncratic sexual interests most of the world didn't dream existed: amputee pin-ups, Tijuana-style bestiality, even crisply and artistically rendered coprophilia. "Crazy what gets people going, ain't it?" Tessler said.

"Where do you get the stockings? My wife'd kill for a pair."

"It ain't easy. There's a black market here in Kansas City, too, and brother I tell you I pay through the nose for the goddamn things. But for some reason you can't sell the weird stuff without 'em."

"There's a gal I'm here to see, and she's a little sore at me right now. Pair of nylons would really fix things up with her."

"Huh. I can send you down to see a man about that. Can't guarantee he'll deliver, but you can try."

We arranged for him to get a set of glossies from folders one and two to Lester on approval, and I left the studio with the address of the man with the hosiery. I'd turned down with some regret Tessler's offer to watch the filming of a stag in the afternoon, but I didn't know how long I'd be in town. Maybe I'd come back tomorrow and have a gander at the process.

I TOOK THE bus downtown. There was a very pretty redhead seated across the aisle from me, and she gave me such a warm and inviting smile that I nearly moved over to try and pick her up. But I reminded myself that I was here to see Vickie, not to accost strange women on public transportation. She crossed her bare legs and I chuckled inwardly at the thought that the stockings I was about to procure for Vickie were probably all it would take to separate the redhead's pretty knees.

I rang the buzzer at the warehouse according to the code indicated: one, three, two. Presently an obese Negro wearing a banker's pinstripes and a grey fedora to match opened the door.

"Merle Tessler sent me," I said.

"That so. What makes you think I know who that is?"

"He said to tell you the soup is in the cans, whatever that means."

He laughed, a genuine and hearty guffaw. "Come on in, tell me what it is I can set you up with. I'm Dewey."

The warehouse was immense and only half full, but it contained rare treasures. There were stacks of tires, and to my left sat a half-dozen brand new adding machines. Above those was a shelf full of Smith Coronas, pre-war models that looked as though they'd never even been beribboned. There were stacks and stacks of shoeboxes on one wall reaching almost to the ceiling, with ladders mounted on rollers and rails to maneuver from one top shelf to another.

"Holy moley," I said. "Take a look at that."

"Yeah, we got a lot of merchandise. If Tessler says you okay we can do business. What you after, exactly?"

"Said you could sell me some nylons for my girl."

"Nylons, sure. Would she like silk better?"

"I guess she would."

"How many pair?"

I thought two pair for Vickie would about get me in the door, and another couple pair for Sally might get me out of the doghouse when I got back to Wichita. Dewey got me what I needed and I paid his exorbitant fee gladly in cash. "Thanks," I said.

"That's all right. You come on back any time. Merle says you okay, that's good enough for me. You work with him on those fuck movies?"

"No, but I used to sell his dirty pictures when I was in the army."

"Yeah? You a supply sarge?"

"That's right. Work for Collins Aircraft down in Wichita now. Or at least I did until last night."

"Do a lot of business with quartermasters. Got a lot of shit to get overseas."

"I know someone just getting started up." I wrote down Lester's information and handed it to Dewey. "He's a good man, just got to Japan from the European theater."

Looking around at all that illegitimate booty I started to get a warm, nostalgic feeling. Here was a man whose business was finding out what people wanted but couldn't get, finding out how to get some of it, and peddling it to the delighted customer at an exorbitant markup. There was creativity in this, and adventure, even a sense of fun. If staying in Wichita as husband and father was my inevitable fate, how much sweeter would it be if I were running this type of operation? "I don't suppose you could use a man down in Wichita?"

"No," he said. "The whole black market's winding down with the war over. Shit, next year there'll be new cars rolling off the line in Detroit and nylons in the department stores and no one'll even remember rationing. Anyway we never had too much luck down in Wichita. You know who Stan Gerard is?"

"I know the name," I said, though in fact I'd met him once in my youth and had made, sorry to say, a bad impression.

"Well, he runs this whole operation up here and a few things down in Wichita. The problem with Wichita is every time you get something good set up, the local competition drops a dime on it. We had a man there last year selling skag in a hotel downtown; first thing you know is some local pusherman called the cops. That's a real low class of crook you got down there."

"Mr. Gerard still doing okay after Boss Pendergast dropped?"

"Hell, yes. There's always somebody to play ball with. Never be another Pendergast, though. You hear Harry Truman hisself went to the funeral? He was still vice president then and there was some people complained and he said 'Tom Pendergast was a friend of mine and I was a friend of his.' That's class, in my book."

Vickie was impressed when I handed her the stockings that afternoon a little before five. "Jesus, Wayne, and here I was all set to read you the riot act for being an unpredictable son of a bitch."

"Go put on a pair and we'll go dancing."

A light snow was coming down when we left the apartment. We danced to the Frankie Masters Orchestra at the Phillips hotel downtown, then got a table in the dining room. Over dinner she talked about hospital politics and a tentative plan she had about moving to Minneapolis for a job at a nursing school.

"What about the doctor?"

"Which?" she said.

"The one you're married to."

"Oh." For just a second she looked uncomfortable, as if she'd been caught doing something wrong. "He doesn't have any immediate plans to come home, so I'm not including him in my decisions."

"Thinking about filing?"

She chewed the bite in her mouth very slowly before responding. "I don't really believe in divorce."

"You're not Catholic, are you?"

"No. I just don't believe in it."

I watched her methodical dissection of her KC strip and wondered what it would be like being married to a really smart woman. Sally was a-one in the looks department but she'd come up a little short intellectually, raised in a house where no one ever read a book. Vickie was as intelligent and educated as I was, more so in some areas. She didn't take any guff, either.

We talked for a while about the orchestra—neither one of us had thought much of it—and the state of the world, and then she asked me point blank why I was there without any advance notice.

"I got fired."

"Fired? Jesus."

"It's nothing, the old souse doesn't even remember he did it, probably. But this lets me put the fear of God into him. Might tell him I had some job offers up here."

She raised an eyebrow. "I'll bet you could find something here if you really wanted."

"Maybe. I talked with a fellow today who runs a photo studio."

"I didn't know you were interested in photography."

"Sure I am. Thinking about ways to make money at it."

"Like open up a portrait studio, shoot weddings, things like that?"

"Things like that, yeah."

SEVERAL HOURS LATER we were lying in her bed, exhausted. After the first time I lay there for twenty minutes and felt the urge again, and to my surprise, an hour or so after that the need arose again. After that one, in the dim lamplight of her bedroom, diffused through the sheets as if through a scrim, I took a good look at her and tried to figure out how she got to me the way she did. Her face was long enough to qualify as horsy, with a nose to proportion, ever so slightly bulbous and two or three degrees off-true to the left; her teeth were a little too prominent, her lower incisors an ivory jumble, and with her hair up her ears looked like saucers. There was no denying, though, that she got me going in a way few others ever had.

"Jesus, it's still freezing in here," she said.

She jumped out of bed stark naked and ran in short quick steps to the hall closet. After a moment's clattering and the sound of something heavy tumbling to the hardwood she came back into the room with an electric space heater. Crouched down on the bedroom carpet, tits aquiver, she plugged it into the wall and closed the door to the hallway. Then she took a flying leap back onto the bed and dug under the covers, pulling herself close to me, shivering so hard I wondered if she was playacting.

"Holy shit it's cold. Something's wrong with that radiator."

"You know those space heaters are a fire hazard."

"I know."

"You ever see what's left of a human body after a housefire?" I said.

"I'm a nurse, Wayne. I've seen stuff that'd curl the hair on your balls. Wouldn't it be romantic, though, going out together like that." Her breasts were pressed against my chest, warm as buns from the oven.

"Sure, burned to a crisp, just bone and ash and suet. Just like in the movies."

"Our skulls'd crack open from the heat," she said, a note of real excitement entering her voice. "And they'd find us in the ruins, locked in an embrace, still smoldering. It'd take them a long time to figure out who you used to be, I bet," she said.

"My wife's having a baby," I said without really planning to.

She nodded. "You didn't tell me that before."

"Thought you might not let me stay."

"You're right about that, but you're forgiven this time," she yawned, and she turned out the light and kissed me, and though we stayed quiet after that it was a long time before I managed to get to sleep.

SEVEN

TWO CAN LIVE
AS CHEAPLY AS ONE

THE WHOLE TIME I knew her, which is to say the last ten years of her life, Sally's mother had an awful odor that clung to her like a shroud, as though she'd never learned to wash properly, or had stopped caring at some point. I didn't see how Sally's father stood it, in fact had trouble picturing how Sally had ever been conceived. If Mr. Tate had endured some sort of brain injury that had removed his olfactory sense I hadn't heard about it.

Neither she nor her husband displayed much affect at all, even when provoked. I could remember one night in high school when Sally and I got drunk and stayed out until four-thirty in the morning. We got home to find them waiting in the parlor, fully dressed, as though they were always up and Sally always out at that hour.

Sally, on the other hand, was a model of personal hygiene, especially after I introduced her to the thrill of muff diving. She was never shy about displaying her emotions, either; many's the time she threw me out of her house for some slight I didn't even know I'd committed. I taught her salty language and how to tell a dirty joke, and though I never made a reader or a scholar out of her she seemed an otherwise perfect mate when I married her at twenty-three, shortly after my graduation from Wichita U.

Something had changed while I was off to war. Her parents were dead, of course, but I sensed there was relief in that, at least inasmuch as she'd never again have to watch a friend pretending not to notice the old girl's piquant ichthyological bouquet. My own mother's homey qualities may have leached into her over the duration, but one of my first acts on returning was to treat my no longer blushing bride to four years' worth of the filthiest jokes the Army could drill into a man, and she laughed so hard she had to change her underwear. And for those first months she was right along with me the way she used to be. I was out with her as many nights for fun as I was with old man Collins for the sake of the job.

It wasn't the war years that changed her, then. It was the little intruder gestating in her belly. I thought long and hard about what Dr. Groff had told me about those chemical and hormonal changes, and I suspected that when the baby abandoned its claim on Sally's womb the natural urges and imperatives of motherhood would counteract the waning of those chemical changes as her body returned to its normal state. In other words, her transformation to simpering homebody risked being permanent.

Her capacity for anger returned, however. I was almost grateful to see the old spitfire resurrected when I walked into the apartment on my return from KC. There was shrieking and crockery was thrown—just a coffee cup, but a nice Maggie-and-Jiggs touch—and a detailed discourse on what a rotten son of a bitch I was to leave her alone with no way to reach me. It turned out that the whole time I was gone Millie Grau was trying to get hold of me, and was very surprised to be told that Mr. Collins had sent me on a business trip. While Sally railed at me, I stuffed the message into my shirt pocket. Maybe when I walked back into Collins's office I'd have a job offer to scare him with.

"You get right on the horn and tell the old man you're sorry you disappeared. You have a wife and a baby to support."

"First of all," I told her, "I'll tell him whatever I damned please. Second, I don't have a baby yet." I proceeded to explain to her my theory about the change in her behavior, and suggested that I knew people who could take care of the situation for us if we wanted to return things to the way they'd been before the war, when we were happy.

Her weapon this time was a cast-iron skillet that had belonged to her mother. Even though it just clipped the back of my skull it drew blood; curiously, this got me no sympathy. I retreated and with Sally screaming obscenities and threats from our open door I ran down the building's main staircase to the street, where I hopped into the Olds and headed straight for the Eaton Hotel, where I got a four-dollar room for the night. This, I suspected, was not going to blow over without my eating a lot of crow.

IN THE MORNING I went to see Dr. Groff again. He didn't seem surprised to see me back so soon.

"I want to know if there's any way to induce an abortion without the woman knowing."

"Use your head, Ogden, how's she supposed to not know she's not pregnant any more?"

"I mean is there a way to do it so it looks like a miscarriage?"

He shook his head, scowling. "Nope. None that I'll be part of. I've done my share of angelmaking, but never without it being the woman's express wish. I don't know of any other doctor who'll do such a thing either." He drew back and his expression softened. "Listen, you're a nervous first timer, it's understandable you get crazy ideas. Don't worry about it, things won't change as much as all that. Look at it this way: every single ancestor of yours back to Adam and Eve did it. Why should you be the one to break the chain?"

I WENT STRAIGHT to my office and found another envelope addressed to DWAYNE OGDUNN on my desk. I put it into the cardboard grocery box I'd brought along with me and started cleaning out the desk for dramatic effect. Mrs. Caspian immediately dialed Miss Grau, without having spoken a word of greeting. My intention was to empty the desk and get out, the better to leverage my position, but as I was on my way out with the desk's meager contents I found Herman Park blocking my path.

"You need to come with me, Mr. Ogden."

"I'm going home," I said.

"You're coming with me to see Mr. Collins at his house, on his orders. Now you've treated me decent, Mr. Ogden, and I've got no itch to hurt you, but Mr. Collins said I was to go ahead if that was the only way."

"Let me follow you in my car."

"You don't have a car. The one you drove in on belongs to Collins aircraft, and if you want to drive off with it later you'd better see the old man now."

WE GOT INTO another company car, an Olds identical to mine but with a different smell to it, and drove out to the southern part of College Hill. Collins's house was large even by the standards of the neighborhood, a three-story colonnaded stone house on an enormous wooded lot. A frail, white-haired maid who looked too old to be in service answered the door and led us in to see Collins. As we passed through the ornately decorated foyer—Oriental antiques of jade and brass on an oak chest, an enormous full-length oil portrait of old Everett in jodhpurs with his goggles hanging around his neck, a burbling fountain with a statue of a spitting nymph—I caught a glimpse of one of Mrs. Collins's paranoiac eyes staring at us from an open sliver of a sliding door. Having met my gaze she slammed the door shut with surprising vigor and produced a solid bang.

Collins was upstairs in his room, under the covers with the lights out, when the maid led us in. "He's expecting you," she said.

"Mr. Collins?" Park said. "Here with Ogden."

Collins mumbled something incomprehensible from his blanket.

"What's that, sir?" Park said.

Collins shouted and thrashed. "Medicine, goddamnit, did he bring the fucking medicine?"

Park looked at me in a half-panic, having evidently failed to understand that I had a mission to accomplish before I was brought into the mighty presence of the Great One.

"What medicine is that, Everett?" I asked. It was the first time I'd ever dared to use his first name to his face.

"You know goddamn well what medicine," he said, saliva flying.

"Don't you have a personal physician to take care of such things?"

"He won't give me anything for the pain, says it's not good to keep it up, anyhow I don't even know what it was and goddamnit my ribs hurt."

"Come on, Park, let's go see if we can't get Everett a script for those ribs."

THAT NIGHT, ENSCONCED in my temporary home in the Eaton Hotel, I opened the envelope I'd found earlier in my desk. This time the note was typewritten, badly:

> *You son of a BITCH I know all about you cheat Uncle sam out money and other and if you think your going to get away with it thing again cocksucker. I am a real hard man. So you should start say your payers and get ready to give me all that doh. Bet your sorry now you killed her. Do you think the rules apply to everyone but you*

Whoever he was, he knew me.

EIGHT

A SENTIMENTAL TALE OF WOE

MY HINTING TO the wife that her pregnancy was not necessarily an immutable condition cost me a week at the Eaton Hotel. It also cost me more than seven thousand dollars in the form of a house not far from our apartment, a few blocks west of Hillside and south of Central, not far from Ketteman's bakery and Cardamon's grocery store. I bought it while I was still at the Eaton and Sally still sore at me. When I parked in front of the house and told her it was ours, a bungalow of recent vintage painted white with a comfortable little yard, her sullenness evaporated.

The first thing I did was install a chain-link fence around the back yard. Who knew, maybe when the kid was born I'd get him a dog. Sally flew around that house hanging curtains and directing deliverymen where to put the furniture, and the week we moved in I picked up my mother at her place in Riverside and brought her over for dinner.

She was a little wraith of a woman by then, much older than her fifty-odd years. She'd had a hard time of it since my old man died, and I wanted her to see that she always had a family to cling to.

"It's been so long since I've seen you, Wayne," she said. "Before Christmas, seems like."

"That can't be right," I said.

"No, that's right," Sally said.

"Well it's nice to see you anyway, son," she said. She was cutting a pork chop into infinitesimally tiny bites, as she always did, never taking a bite until the whole piece of meat had been dissected. It used to bother me the way she did that, but now I felt a curious fondness for her odd ways.

I was sore at Sally because I'd brought steaks home from Cardamon's, but she had three big pork chops in the icebox and was determined to fix them for my mother on the grounds that the old bird loved them. Fine, I said, but I bought steaks, good KC strips, and when a man has steak on his mind pork chops aren't a satisfactory substitute. My voice must have been raised because I could see her eyes glistening, so I cupped her chin and kissed her and told her whatever she wanted to make would be swell with me.

After dinner I dropped my mother off at her house. I was still a little out of joint about the steak, so I stopped in at Red's. I hadn't been in in a few weeks; part of my new deal involved giving Park some of my responsibilities, including that of accompanying the old man on his nightly debauches. Of course he would have been present anyway, but the old man liked him better than he'd liked Billy Clark, and Park knew how to ignore a needling remark, which got the old man's goat and earned his respect at the same time.

The scarecrow who loved Barbara the b-girl was tending bar, and as I bellied up there was a reserved hostility in his affectless gaze as he poured me a shot of bourbon and a Schlitz. Just to provoke him I asked if Barbara was around.

"Don't know who you mean," he said.

"Sure you do. She works here as a b-girl, got ants in her pants."

"She's not here." There was emotion choking in his voice and I decided I'd better knock it off. I didn't want to get into a fight, particularly, and I felt a little sorry for the guy anyway. What kind of numbnuts falls in love with a gal like Barbara?

A different b-girl came and sat next to me. I bought her a sidecar and listened to her talk about life in wartime and how hard it was and her husband wasn't even home yet and she sure wished he'd get mustered out so she could get some good loving. This one was younger than Barbara and hadn't passed her prime yet, but her prime wasn't much. She was skinny and hard-faced and wore her makeup wrong. Even by the forgiving light of Red's I could see she had too much rouge on.

It's funny the things you learn in different lines of work. Before I became a pimp I couldn't have cared less about the subject of makeup, but when your livelihood depends on your girls looking their best you develop a keen interest in the subject. This one—Janice by name, if she was to be believed—didn't wear enough eye makeup. She had a mean look to her, and she needed some eye shadow to soften her up.

She asked for another sidecar and I paid for it. The bartender was watching me pretty close, maybe in case I took her out to the parking lot the way I'd done with his beloved. There wasn't much chance of that, though. This one didn't excite me at all, though I found her tales of woe diverting.

As a child her pop had beaten her senseless on a regular basis, and then one day a man came to their house and had a talk with him. The stranger asked little Janice if her old man treated her okay. She was sore at Dad that day because he'd wrenched her little arm for talking back, so she told the man her dad beat her regularly and hard, too.

"What I hear," said the stranger to her old man, "is that this child was put into the hospital with a broken collar bone."

Her father tried to deny it, but little Janice piped up that it was true. "Did he do that, or was it an accident?"

She'd been told to say it was an accident, but something in the stranger's deferential and courteous attitude towards her made her want to tell the truth. Maybe the man would convince her dad that she shouldn't be hit for little things, just the big ones.

So she told him her dad had shoved her down the cellar stairs and made her stay down there in the dark for three hours with the broken collarbone. The stranger got an odd look on his face, sort of a smile and sort of a grimace, and then he proceeded to beat her father to death with his bare fists before her horrified eight-year-old eyes.

Turns out, she told me, the stranger was her real father, just out of jail for manslaughter, and he went looking for his wife and daughter and, asking around town, heard his wife was shacked up with a mean, mean man who was beating up the little girl. Her real father went to jail for a real long time for that; he was lucky he wasn't hanged.

Or so she told the story. It was rehearsed to the point she probably didn't know any more how much if any of it was true. I asked her where it happened and she told me Ohio, near Chilicothe, but she pronounced it wrong. I didn't correct her, just bought her a third drink and went over to watch a couple of fellows in denim overalls playing pinball. One of them, a wiry farm boy who to me looked high on amphetamines, was winning a fair amount of money. Someone had done a piss-poor job of cutting the kid's hair, leaving his temple nearly bare on the left side and a quarter-inch thick on the right. His friend's head was buzz-cut to semi-baldness, and the friend watched the pinball's cascading and careening with something like a sense of grief. The skinny pinball fiend was in an antic trance as he rocked the machine and caressed its lower corners, manipulating the flippers as expertly as the tailgunner on a B-29.

A powerful blow landed between my shoulder blades and propelled me forward and into the pinball hustler, whose machine clanged, a red TILT sign lighting on the board.

"Son of a bitch," the kid said, and I was afraid I was going to have to fight three people when I saw the farm boys drop their belligerent stances. Over my shoulder I saw someone vaguely familiar and realized that the blow had come without malicious intent, or at least malice consciously aimed at me.

"Rackey?"

He was beaming and extending his hand for a shake. "Mr. Ogden, it sure is good to see you."

He didn't seem to grasp that he'd queered the kid's pinball game, and the two farmboys were getting set up for another game, acting as though they were unaware of our very presence. "How are you? How's that job on the line working out?"

"Real good. I don't like the foreman much, and I'm liable to pop that shop steward's head right off his neck one of these days, but hell, at least I'm working."

We adjourned to the bar and stood discussing his wife's continued perfidy over a couple of drinks. The bartender liked Rackey even less than he did me, which made me wonder what mayhem my protégé might have wrought here in the past.

"I'm sure she ain't fucking my brother any more, 'cause I broke both his arms and told him stay the shit away from my house and my wife. Now my mom and pop are sore at me along with him and the wife."

"Rough," I said.

"You said it. At least the wife's not straying any more."

"That's good," I said in as neutral a tone as I could manage, wanting neither to egg him on to further violence nor to suggest any sort of disapproval on my part.

"She knows damn well anybody she messes with is gonna bleed."

"Uh-huh."

"You know, things are a little better with her since you got me that job, though."

"I'm glad to hear that."

Janice the b-girl had been watching us from her post down the bar. At length she arose and sashayed over to us on her skinny legs.

"How's about introducing me to your big strapping friend, Wayne?" she said. I didn't remember telling her my name, but what the hell.

He stuck his hand out. "Elmer Rackey."

"I'm Janice," she said as I signaled the bartender to bring her a drink. When he brought it I saw him looking at her in a pinched, hateful way and it struck me that he looked at everybody that way except for his idolized, roundheeled Barbara.

By that point Janice was well into another well-polished apocryphal anecdote featuring herself as the central sufferer. This one involved having her broken-down old Ford stolen right after she'd filled it up, and having it recovered by the police with its tank empty.

"That was a whole week's ration of gas, Elmer. Lordy, I asked those cops how I could get the gas replaced, meaning was there some way I could get the ration stamps replaced legit, you know? And this big mean cop says to me, 'you try it, lady, you'll spend the rest of the war in the can, 'cause we don't take to black marketeers here in Wichita.' Can you imagine saying that to a poor woman who's just lost her whole week's ration of gas? I had to walk to work all week except when I caught a ride with a girlfriend."

"Wish't I could get my hands on the dirty son of a bitch that stole it, that's all I can say," Rackey said, the last clause barely audible. There was a murderous, distant glint in his eyes that gave me pause and made me consider once again how to keep this guy out of trouble until the day I might need him.

SALLY WAS ASLEEP when I got in, the dinner dishes drying in the rack next to the sink. By the light of a brand new lamp I sat in my dad's favorite chair and read through a manuscript my grandfather had left him, an autobiography whose details and generalities I was unable to verify or credit, though I had heard him tell some of the same stories on his various visits. It was like listening to him talk, though, and the unpublishable randiness of the thing corresponded with my memories of him. In the early thirties he caused a scandal when, staying with us for the summer, he embarked on a liaison with a married, fortyish cashier at the Orpheum theater, an undeniably attractive redheaded woman with a pronounced lisp but no other obvious debilities. He was around ninety at the time and quite proud of the fact that her husband had threatened to kill him and never made good on the threat.

THAT ANONYMOUS PEN pal of mine was right about at least one thing: I had made a nice illicit bundle off of Uncle Sam. In the little safe in the basement that contained among other things my discharge papers and my Purple Heart—probably the only one ever awarded for getting stabbed by a rival pimp—was a whole lot of illicit cash I'd managed to smuggle back from Europe. The army doesn't make that easy, believe me, but if anybody has an edge in that domain it's a supply sergeant. I wasn't able to bring it all; not to toot my own horn, but I wasn't as greedy as all that anyway. I let the whores have some of it, in hopes they could band together and find a protector more worthy of them than my predecessor had been. I was busy with the combination, preparing to replace my grandfather's manuscript inside, when the door above the stairs creaked open, startling a sharp intake of breath and an audible gasp from me.

"Wayne, sweetie?"

"Uh-huh."

"Just wondering if that was you down there."

Annoyed at the interruption, and a little red-faced at having the shit scared out of me like that, I snapped. "Coming down to check was foolish. If it hadn't been me, then it would have been a burglar. You could have been raped or killed."

She didn't react the way she'd been doing lately. Instead she came downstairs and put her soft, cool white hand on my cheek. "Are you doing okay, honey? I know you don't really like the work at Collins."

Her solicitousness caught me off my guard, and I stammered a reply to the effect that I was perfectly happy working there, that I'd do anything for her and the baby.

"I was just thinking tonight how much you always wanted to be a pilot," she said.

"That was a long time ago."

"But I know you still think about it. Would you like to take flying lessons?" she asked. "I'm sure you could get some kind of cut rate, working for Collins."

It was sweet of her, wrong though she was. I stood and kissed her. "You go on to bed, now, and I'll be up in a minute."

She climbed the stairs, turning once to give me a loving, blushing look over her shoulder, and I resumed opening the lock.

The amount inside was a little over five thousand dollars, and I hadn't yet spent a dime of it, not even on the down payment on the house. It was unworthy of me and I knew it, but the nagging fear that my dear wife might somehow get into the safe weighed upon me. The poison pen-man must have designs on the money, too, and despite my determination not to let the little shit get the better of me, I resolved to go to the Third National Bank downtown in the morning and rent a safety deposit box.

MAYBE IT WOULD have been wisest to wean Collins off the dope at that early stage, but I wasn't about to give up the advantage I held over him. His own physician wouldn't have allowed him opiates except under hospital conditions, and he was too well-known in Wichita to risk approaching another doctor. And cagey and evil though the old bastard was, he didn't have the specific, hard-won skills necessary to procure illicit goods without consequence.

But Groff was getting nervous about dispensing the volume of Hycodan that Collins now required—already there was one weekly prescription in my name and one in Park's—and he gave me the name of a Dr. Briggs who would show great empathy for a man enduring the chronic pain of broken ribs, particularly a man as wealthy and well-connected as Everett Collins.

I met Dr. Briggs at his office in the same downtown building that housed my dentist's surgery. He was about sixty years old, with receding salt and pepper hair, black, round-framed eyeglasses and a leering smile. He was only too glad to fill my prescription, and another in the name of Herman Park. "How about methadone?" he asked. "Has he tried anything beyond Hycodan? Lot of doctors, Groff among them, have an awful lot of faith in whatever's the newest drug on the market, but some of the old ones are better, if you ask this old sawbones." He went on to rhapsodize about the effects of this braintickler and that one, to the point that I began to wonder how the old coot had managed to hang onto his license to practice medicine all these years.

I promised him I'd ask the old man to think about it and headed for the nearest Rexall to fill the script. After reading the prescription, the druggist appraised me in a manner that bordered on disrespect, and though I affected not to notice I made a mental note to skip this particular pharmacy in the future.

When I dropped off the pills I stopped for a chat with Millie Grau, who had been treating me like the greatest thing to hit Collins Aircraft Company since the introduction of the Airmaster. "Mr. Collins just wasn't himself while you were gone. I don't know exactly what happened last week but I guess he got drunk and fired you again, didn't he?"

"Something like that," I said.

"I wish he'd quit that drinking, he does things he regrets so often now."

"How's that?"

"Firing you, firing Mr. Cook."

"I took it upon myself to fire Mr. Cook while Mr. Collins was convalescent."

"Well, things like that. And I guess you know about poor Miss Gladstone from the secretarial pool."

"Doesn't ring a bell."

She looked down at her shoes, flushing. I looked down too, though my focus was on her legs. "The girl who had to go away to Kansas City for a week. None of that would have ever happened but for his drinking. I've been praying so hard, but you know what? He has to want to stop on his own."

I was newly impressed with Miss Grau. I'd always thought of her as a very pleasant and desirable girl, but I'd never attributed much to her in the way of smarts or insight. She was clearly the one person on earth the boss confided in, the only soul in all creation to whom he felt able to confess his multitude of shames and vulnerabilities. I hadn't suspected the old boy still had that capacity; she was the last, tenuous connection between Everett Collins and the human race.

NINE
THE
ENEMIES LIST

I WAS SPENDING A little more time around the plant in the daytime and letting Herman Park take up a little bit more of the slack at night, preferring to carouse on my own, and the old man had picked up on the fact that I wasn't around as much on his nocturnal excursions.

"What the hell are you hanging around here in the daytime for? That's not what I pay you to do."

"Thought it might be good to spend some time around the house in the evening, what with the wife expecting and all."

He grunted and frowned. "I'm taking some flack for keeping you on, you know."

He leaned back in his big leather chair and picked up one of the wooden models on his desk, an early Airmaster with black fuselage and golden wings. He moved it through the air, following it with his eyes and making a sputtering engine sound, the opiates having rendered him so boyish that it was hard to hate him, almost.

"That's good of you," I said.

"It's Huff and that crowd on the board that's been trying to replace me with the Missus. They think you're a bad influence on me." Down towards the carpet the Airmaster dove, saved at the last minute from disaster by the sure hand of its designer, who performed a couple of tricky loops on the way back skyward, still making that engine sound in the back of his throat. "And you're paid too much versus what you actually do around here. You have some enemies in your own department, you know."

"Mrs. Caspian," I said.

"Nah, the big gal likes you, she's the one who's headed off an open rebellion down there."

I was stunned to learn this about Mrs. Caspian, who'd never addressed a civil or unnecessary word to me in the entire time I'd known her. "I thought they all liked me okay down there."

"There's someone else they figure should be department head. I was thinking maybe I'd transfer you."

"It'd be the same any place else. The fact is I ought to be on your personal payroll and not the company's, but it's your company and you run it the way you see fit."

"You got that right, boy. Anyway, watch yourself around Huff."

"Hell, I don't even know him."

"Doesn't matter. He's the comptroller, he knows what you make, and he hears what goes on in your department. Which is pretty damned irregular. Thing is, see, Huff would love to see me carted out of here in a straitjacket so's he could run the financial side his way, but that's not going to happen, is it?" He brought the Airmaster down onto his desk for a perfect three-point landing, and I was impressed to note that its Lilliputian tires actually spun.

"How do you know all this?"

"Miss Grau keeps her ears open and tells me everything there is to know around this godforsaken place. Everybody talks to her, and a lot of people figure she probably doesn't like you because you're a bad seed and encourage my degenerate tendencies." He laughed, as if that were the most ridiculous idea he'd come across all week.

I DROVE TO Stanley's at Kellogg and Oliver and ordered a cup of coffee from a heavy, slouching waitress whose weak chin managed some sort of structural alchemy that made her wide face rather pretty. She stared at me after she brought the coffee, her manner neither hostile nor flirtatious, just curious. I did my best to ignore her as I wrote down a list of my known nemeses on a yellow legal pad.

I started with all the men in my department, and parenthetically added Mrs. Caspian to the list, albeit with a pang of guilt after hearing that she'd stood up for me. Until I could verify that, though, I would treat her as a possible quisling, just like everyone in the Publicity and Marketing Department.

Then I wrote down the name of Ernest J. Huff, the comptroller. I added the three members of the Board of Directors with whom he was allied: Mr. J.T. Burress, Mr. Wilbur Lamarr, and Mr. George Latham. The four of them had opposed Collins on matters of wartime production and postwar retooling, and I assumed they were the ones trying to replace the old man with his compliant wife. I put Mrs. Collins on there, too, just for the hell of it.

The waitress refilled my coffee cup and I asked her for a glazed donut to match her eyes. I added Hiram Fish to my list, not because he
posed any real threat to me or the boss but because he was a fink who
looked like a gigolo. I added Billy Clark because he'd stirred up all the
trouble that ended up with the boss on narcotics, which was turning
out to be a pain in the balls.

The waitress brought my donut and kept looking at me. Finally
she spoke.

"Did you go to WU around '36, '37?"

"I sure did," I said.

She grinned, and though it made her look familiar I still couldn't
place her. "Duane something?"

"Wayne."

"That's it! Remember me? Wanda Blythe? We had Biology together."

I affected a look of joy. "Wanda, swell to see you." Dear God,
though, it wasn't. I remembered her well, a lovely, charming sylph of
a girl, possessed of a melodious giggle and a tendency to blush, and in
my college years I wanted badly to get her into bed.

"Did you marry that girl? Was it Sarah?"

"Sally. Yeah, we're married and she's expecting our first."

"Your first? After all these years? Gosh, I'm on my fifth already."
She patted her belly. "Pretty soon I'll have to stop working on my feet
and cashier until it comes."

The idea that the young beauty I'd lusted after no longer existed
hit me harder than I would have imagined. A sadness overtook me, a
sense that the world I'd known was disappearing, decaying before my
eyes, and I asked her to give me the donut in a bag.

"It's for Sally," I said. "Cravings."

I ATE THE donut in the car on the way to Red's. The sullen, self-pitying bartender wasn't on the premises tonight, but there sat his cherished Barbara, looking more pie-eyed than usual. I wondered if Red had ever been told that the whole principle behind the b-girl system is feeding them watered-down drinks so they can keep cockteasing all night long without getting shitfaced and saying the hell with it and stumbling off to the parking lot with whatever charmer is lucky enough to get her to that exact level of inebriation.

Red Garnett was there tonight, sitting in a booth with a peroxide blonde who looked as drunk as Barbara did. Younger than Barbara, she looked rode hard and put up wet. When I went over to say hello I addressed Red only.

"How are you, Ogden? You working for the old flyboy any more? Never see you in here with him and that bodyguard."

"I still am, just a different set of responsibilities now. Not so much babysitting."

"Uh-huh. I heard about those responsibilities." Red gave a low, rueful laugh. His hair wasn't very red anymore but he still had most of it, and he reached back with his hand and smoothed down a cowlick. "Many's the gal I've had to let go around here when they developed the habit. Methadone, is it?"

"No idea what you're talking about, Red," I said.

"Sure you don't. Every time he comes in he's goofy, the son of a bitch. You listen to me, you best get him off that stuff or you'll find yourself in darktown scoring heroin some Friday midnight."

"Doubt it."

I knew that my failure to acknowledge the blonde's presence would get her goat, and finally she looked straight at me. "Do you mind?" she said. "We were having a private conversation. And I don't care to hear talk about that sort of low business."

"Shut your noisemaker," Red said. "You don't determine what gets discussed." He gestured to her. "Wayne, this here's my wife, Betty."

"Hello, Betty," I said. Red was well over sixty, and despite her haggard appearance this girl wasn't much more than twenty-five.

"You mind what I said now. You can get into trouble peddling scripts. Take it from one who knows."

I sat down at a table by myself where some industrious cracker named FERLIN had applied his energies and skills to carving his name into the wood. No fewer than four Kilroys peered idiotically at me from that same tabletop, and someone named GaLEN had immortalized his love for a DoRothEa. The childishness of the inlay brought my anonymous correspondent to mind, and I felt an unexpected and unaccustomed sense of anxiety at the thought, accentuated by what Red had just said about my activities as a procurer of narcotics.

I set the legal pad down and by the time I got up to go home my list was filigreed with doodled pistols, daggers, skulls, and nooses, and I was no closer to neutralizing my enemies than I'd been before I walked in.

I'D TAKEN TO eating dinner at home on a regular basis, and Sally was making a serious effort to improve her cooking. The three miserable years she spent living in my mother's house while I was in Europe hadn't improved her skills in the kitchen; the old lady was an awful cook who had never cared for food much, possibly due to a head injury sustained when she was a young woman that diminished her sense of smell. Sally's slovenly mother hadn't been much of a cook either; when she was in a depressive trance, which was most of the time, she could hardly summon the wherewithal to throw together a roast chicken. During her occasional two- or three-day spells of frenetic activity, she'd concoct improvised artistic creations that wouldn't have passed muster in the galley of an insane asylum, then cackle with glee at her family's brave attempts to choke them down.

But Sally had noticed that I didn't much like what she cooked, and she bought recipe books, and she was making improvements. She even made me calves' liver and onions once a week, even though that meant she had to make herself a different main course. "It's good for you," I'd tell her, knowing full well the taste and texture nauseated her. "Full of iron. Good for baby," a phrase that got thrown around a lot during those months.

THE CHANGE IN diet made more appealing the prospect of staying at home in the evenings, but one night after a strikingly unsuccessful attempt at a meat loaf—the spices the recipe called for struck her, in her delicate digestive condition, as unappealing, and at the moment it called for an egg to be folded in she realized we had none—I was feeling some hunger pangs and told her I was going out. Though she glared at me over my half-eaten lump of bland ground beef, overcooked to a blackish-grey stiffness, she didn't object.

AND SO THAT evening I followed Park and Collins on their nightly prowl. I wasn't necessarily looking for a woman, but when Collins decided he wanted to get some gals sent up to a room at the Eaton I didn't object. Just like in the old days, I took care of renting the room, calling the fellow who ran the whores, and paying off the front desk.

I also made sure that the hotel detective got a separate payment, and when I poked my head in his office he greeted me like an old army buddy.

"Ogden, where the hell you been keeping yourself?" His pink, hairless head shone under the naked bulb in the overhead socket. The Eaton was still a swell place, but the hotel detective's office belonged in a flophouse, right down to the worn-down trail in the carpet from door to desk and the peeling 1915 wall paper.

"Here and there, Jerry," I said. "Out of trouble, mostly." I handed him an envelope with a sawbuck in it.

"That doesn't sound like the old Wayne. You out on the town with the boss?"

"Yeah, for old times' sake. Got old Herman Nester sending some girls up, just so you know."

"That's fine. Most of Herman's girls are class enough they don't stink up the place. You tell the old man Jerry sends his best."

As per usual we rented a suite for Collins and an adjacent single in case Park or I wanted to take a crack at the other girls. When they arrived I was drinking a Falstaff, Collins a water tumbler full of gin, and Park nothing at all. There were three of them, and as Jerry had indicated, they were high class by the standards of Wichita whores, neatly coiffed and dressed as fashionably as any outcall girls I'd seen. Collins was all over the first gal, groping her and pinning her to the couch while the rest of us sat quietly, waiting for him to make up his mind which girl he was going to fuck. He got up off of the first one, a patient, unflappable redhead whose makeup and hair were considerably off-kilter, and moved to the second candidate. This one was a big-eyed, moonfaced blonde with a slight resemblance to Joan Blondell, and I was hoping Collins would settle on the third because I had always wanted to put the pork to Joan Blondell. Collins pulled her to her feet and backed her up to the wall, and she reached around and grabbed his ass and kissed him before he had a chance to move in. The old pervert was taken aback; he didn't like aggressive girls as a rule. He pushed her to the wall again and pulled himself away, pirouetting inadvertently back onto the couch with a thud, right next to girl number three, another blonde. This one was a phony, and her features were so thin she looked a little like a ferret, but her makeup was applied professionally and to a drunkard's eye she looked fine. Add to that her sly, eager smile and we had ourselves a winner.

While she and the boss adjourned to the bedroom I offered Park first dibs on the room next door. "No, thanks," he said. "Got in a hell of a lot of trouble last time. Penicillin kind of trouble."

Another rule I learned in the pimping trade: When screwing professional or semi-professional women, a prophylactic is always advisable. I didn't say that to Park, though, since I was pretty anxious to get to that other room myself.

IN THE ADJOINING room the blonde call girl asked me if I wanted to undress her or watch her do it. I told her to go ahead and asked if she was up for an ass reaming.

"Sure, it's ten dollars extra. You'll have to go out for some Vaseline, though, I didn't bring any. Also I need to be awful relaxed, so I'm gonna be needing my pussy eaten first."

"Fine by me," I said.

"I just mention it because a lot of guys won't."

"I'm not one of 'em." I put my jacket on and poured her a drink. "I'll hit the drug store and be back in a few."

THE ALL-NIGHT DRUG store was just a few blocks away. Ten minutes later the clerk was ringing up the Vaseline, but not without trying to sell me on some Mentholatum instead. He was about twenty-two or three with too much grease in his hair, working too hard at being helpful.

"Most everything you can use the one for you can use the other. And it was invented right here in Wichita, did you know that? Plus it's got the cooling menthol."

"That's the thing," I said. "I don't think the whore in question wants her asshole mentholated."

His face went blank for a second, then he looked away with his mouth wide and without managing to meet my gaze again dropped the Vaseline in the paper sack.

BACK AT THE room the call girl was taking a bath with the bathroom door open. "I can come out any time," she said. "This helps me relax beforehand."

"Fine with me," I said, watching her under the water.

"My hole's already clean. Had a client wanted some yesterday and I haven't had a BM since, so you're in luck. You might have had to buy a douche bag, too."

"I've always been lucky."

"What's your name?" She closed her eyes and slid down further under the water, her chest rising up slightly so that her nipples surfaced like big brown periscopes.

"Wayne."

"Pleased to meet you, Wayne. I'm Irma."

"Irma."

"How'd you get interested in butt sex, Wayne?"

"High school. Had a girl wouldn't do it the regular way."

"Saving it, huh? I don't exactly get that, but my sister's that same way."

"I only get a hankering for it every once in a while, but the wife's knocked up and she won't do it. Here's hoping that's temporary."

"If it ain't you know where to call."

I SPENT A good fifteen minutes on cuntlapping, and then we got down to business. She was plenty relaxed by then, and her interior muscle control would have done a yogi proud. I was disciplined enough to get a good ten minutes out of her, though, and when I flopped down beside her afterward she had a peculiar smile on her face, like she'd just gotten away with some foul deed.

"I'll tell you the honest truth, Wayne," she said. "I like that just fine myself once in a while."

WHEN I GOT back to the suite I found the old man sitting in an easy chair looking waxy and embalmed, staring straight ahead, and for a split second I wondered how he could be dead and still sitting up. Then he turned his head toward me.

"Ogden," he said, voice sepulchral and strangling, "you have to help me."

"Help you what?"

"Find me a doctor. Not my doctor. Not Pendleton, he can't know about this."

"What's the matter?"

"It wouldn't work, Ogden."

"What wouldn't?"

"Jesus Christ on a pogo stick, what do you think I'm talking about?" He gestured toward the bedroom with his thumb, old yellow teeth bared and tears in his eyes. "It just wouldn't stand up. You have to find me a sawbones to fix this." He turned to the blonde whore, who was sitting with her redheaded friend on the couch. "And you, if you ever breathe a word of this I'll have your tits cut off."

"I'll never breathe a word, sweetie. Anyway, believe me, it happens to every guy."

"I'm sixty-three goddamn years old, I've had sexual intercourse at least once a day since I was seventeen and it has never, ever happened to me." It was hard to tell whether the breaking in his voice was from rage or self-pity.

"You come see me again, you'll do fine next time. I think you're cute."

"Well I think you're a succubus. I think you stole the lead out of my pencil." He stood up, pointing at her, and then he sat back down. He turned to Park. "Get the car, Herman."

I ELECTED TO walk. It wasn't that far, and it was a pleasant evening, getting warm with a clear sky and the stars thick as bedbugs. I picked up an *Evening Beacon* out of a machine on my way out and walked with it under my arm, thinking about Irma. That had been the best sexual experience I'd had since Italy, where one of my girls—as it happens, the one I got knifed over—had such exquisite muscle control that her colleagues charged half price on the nights she worked. Otherwise they wouldn't have had any johns at all, so eager were the GIs to get a crack at the average-looking Giovanna. I learned an important lesson with those gals, that looks could sometimes come in second to personality and sexual experience and, occasionally, to anatomical idiosyncrasy. Not that I ever intended to pimp again, but speaking purely as a client I thought I had a leg up on my competing johns.

I got home and turned on the lamp and read the paper in the easy chair. On the front page was a photograph of a wife-killer getting taken into custody. His name was Bensen, a shop steward on the line over at Beechcraft, which meant he'd spent the war at home. Some guys were glad about that circumstance—getting classed 4-F, or having a militarily essential job—and some let it stick in their craw until they felt like they had something to prove. What struck me about the photo wasn't the disheveled look of the skinny murderer, with his blood-stained undershirt and wild, greasy hair, but the expression of horrified surprise on his face as he found himself staring into the camera lens, as though the worst part of the day so far hadn't been the realization that he'd gone too far and actually beaten his long-suffering Harriett to death, nor had it been his arrest (which, judging by his bloody lip, had also involved a walloping from the arresting officers). No, Bensen looked as though the worst of it was being ambushed by the *Beacon*'s photographer, the explosion of the tiny bulb in its round, silvered reflector, the worst day of his life forever enshrined in a morgue drawer of Wichita's finest scandal sheet. The look was that of a public shaming; that look was why our Pilgrim forebears invented the stocks.

I knew my way around a camera. My grandfather's work in photography had proceeded from the wet plate era to the first years of Kodachrome, and he had passed the rudiments of the trade on to me. I didn't own a camera any more, but that night I started thinking about the possibilities. After all, I would certainly be needing a camera soon to record the first years of the baby's life. Besides, who knew what kind of clandestine photographs a sly and resourceful shutterbug might be able to get, if he knew enough about his subjects' habits and comings and goings?

THE NEXT MORNING before office hours I called Ezra Groff and arranged to bring Collins in for an early visit. When we arrived, Collins had on dark glasses and an old black overcoat of my own whose arms were a little short for him and a black slouch hat. He was addled that morning and, for the first time since I'd known him, seemed actually frail.

Groff was his usual curt self, but I could tell he was impressed to have such a luminary in his office. I offered to leave the room but Collins wanted me there. We sat across the desk from the doctor, who made a steeple of his fingers and nodded, frowning, at everything Collins said.

"I don't believe you," Groff said when the old man repeated his boast of having gotten laid every day of his adult life.

"Well, damn near anyway. Some days more than once so it amounts to the same thing."

Groff shrugged. "And when you're drunk you still manage?"

"Hell, yes."

"And how many prescriptions for Hycodan are you current with?"

Collins looked over at me in search of an answer.

"Four," I said. "But the other three are at higher dosages than the ones you write."

Groff nodded, rubbed his temples, closed his eyes. "Mister Collins, it's a tribute to your virility that this is the first time you've failed to achieve an erection, given the amount of opiates in your system." The eyes popped open. "How are your bowel movements?"

"When I manage to have one these days it's a big one."

"Severe constipation's another symptom."

"Are you telling me I can't have the pills any more?"

"You can have them if you want them. You just have to accept that they have other, unintended effects."

"But if I want to have relations with a girl I have to quit."

"You think about it. Have Mr. Ogden contact me if you want my help."

Outside we got into the car. When I pulled away from the curb he tapped me on the shoulder (he was of course riding in the back seat). "You got any medicine on you? I need to think about this business real hard."

TEN
A GOOD DEAL
IN HOME FURNISHINGS

PARK AND I had taken to sitting around Stanley's late mornings. A couple of able-bodied men could have found other pursuits on a weekday, but it was important the boss be able to find us if he managed to rouse himself sufficiently to roll out of bed and pick up the phone. And so we played gin rummy and read the morning editions of both papers over coffee until lunchtime, after which we drove over to the Collins manse whether summoned or not and did our best to get the old bastard into a fit condition to leave the house and make a showing at the plant, if only to stave off the rumors that had, inevitably, begun to circulate regarding his fitness to lead the company. The rumors mostly involved sickness and senility rather than addiction to opiates, but that time was probably coming before long.

A redhaired man with a lopsided tilt to his head and an extraordinarily long neck came in one day around eleven and sat down at the counter. The counterman that day was an old Dutchman we called Fritz, and he didn't answer much when the man tried to engage him in conversation.

"I'm so worried about the whole business I'm thinking of moving up to Oregon and building a bomb-proof house. Half of 'em died of radiation sickness, did you know that? You'll have to have a house lined with lead."

Fritz stuck to his grill, faced away from the man without answering or even grunting. "Don't let Fritz hurt your feelings, he's just sore because the krauts lost the war," I said.

Fritz spun and pointed his spatula at me like an épée. "Shut your piehole, Ogden, I'm from Holland, you know goddamn well my name's Pier." Then he turned back to the grill again.

The redhead turned to me now. "Do you understand what I'm talking about? We're walking around pretending everything's normal but the fact is the commies are probably working on a bomb right this very minute, and you know where the first one's going to be aimed at? Right here at Wichita, because that's where the aircraft plants are. And who knows where you can go that'd be any safer?"

Park smirked and rolled his eyes, but I just nodded in the fellow's direction. I'd seen guys get like this in the service, monomaniacal and antsy and trying to convince the world of their private obsessive delusion, until the whole thing collapses into despair and sorrow. This guy was headed for a nervous breakdown and no amount of believing him or not would slow him down one little bit.

IT HAD BEEN a couple of weeks since the last letter, and my nameless correspondent was on the move. His latest missive was postmarked

Bismarck, North Dakota, and this time he was brazen enough to write me on stationery from the Bismarck Hotel.

Dear Sarg

What I hear your maried. I sure hope shes a sweet piece
of poontang cause oh buddy Im going to give it to her like
nobodys busness after I kill you dead.

from

your pal

What kind of addlebrained shitbird, I asked myself, writes self-incriminating letters to his intended victim? Either he was an incompetent moron or a bona fide lunatic. In either case he had a fair amount of accurate information about me, and I was wondering where he got it. If he was a relative of one of the girls from Rome I didn't see where he'd get that, but an army man or a vet with good connections might easily find things out. I was thinking maybe I'd make a visit to the VA myself.

ONE AFTERNOON NOT long after that I asked Mrs. Caspian if I might accompany her out to her car. As we walked I realized that her failure to look me in the eye and refusal to speak more than the absolute necessary minimum were not matters of rudeness or contempt but of shyness. In the daylight of the parking lot her face showed bright blushing red, and when I asked her if I had any enemies in the department she turned, met my gaze, and blurted, "Oh, yes, Mr. Ogden, all of them."

The spring daylight revealed something else: Mrs. Caspian was not unattractive at all, her body now appearing to me full and womanly rather than fat, her face expressive and almost pretty. The effect was not unlike that in a movie where a plain girl takes off her glasses and is revealed to be a beauty.

"Is there someplace we can talk alone?"

There was a look of panic in her eyes. She looked down at her shoes as though thinking hard, then looked up. "My apartment." She wrote an address down on a chewing gum wrapper. "Meet me there in an hour."

SHE HAD CHANGED from her business clothes into a light spring dress when I got to her little second-story apartment in Riverside, and there was a tray with a coffee pot and two cups on the coffee table. I sat down in the middle of the couch, thinking there was no way on God's green earth that I was going to seduce this woman, or that she was even up for it. But I had that wonderful feeling you get right before you screw a woman for the first time, that childish anticipation that permeates the air of a room. Very rarely had that feeling failed me, and she sat down next to me rather than in the easy chair and crossed her legs in a way that showed a great deal more of them than I'd seen previously.

"Now Mr. Cave and Mr. Baines, they don't much like your being around but they're just following along. Mr. Kohl and Mr. Linhart, though, they talk about you behind your back all the time. Call you . . . " She could barely bring herself to say it. "They call you 'Old Brown-nose.' I had to ask them what it means. It means . . . "

"I was in the Army, Mrs. Caspian."

"Oh. Of course."

I thought I'd ratchet things up a little and get a better idea of whether she was going to tumble. "Is Mr. Caspian at home?"

"Oh. Well." She was sweating now despite the pleasant breeze coming in through the window, and waved a magazine in front of her face. "He's a salesman, he sells vacuum cleaners, Hoovers, not door to door, he's an official sales rep, and he's got the whole territory of Kansas and northern Oklahoma, too, so of course he makes regular trips to places, in fact he's on the road about three weeks a month, excepting weekends, when mostly he's home."

It was more than she'd said to me since I'd met her. I put my hand on a pudgy, dimpled, pretty knee, leaned in, and kissed her.

Mr. Caspian, it seemed, had not been fulfilling his conjugal duties on a regular enough basis even on those nights when he was home. His wife responded to my pass so enthusiastically that we barely made it to the bedroom. Mrs. Caspian liked it every which way, and she made so much noise I had to ask if the neighbors downstairs would hear.

"They're old and deaf," she said, in between loud yelps.

If she didn't care, I guessed I didn't either. She was a big gal, with a big voice, and afterward I asked her about that.

"Oh, yes, I'm a trained singer. I still sing in the choir at St. Mary's."

"No fooling?"

"I sure am. If you think Collins is bad, you ought to see the backstabbing that goes on in a cathedral choir."

She wasn't the kind of Catholic girl whose sense of guilt made sex more exciting; Mrs. Caspian didn't seem to have any sense of guilt about it at all. She had a look of quiet contentment that was quite at odds with the face she habitually showed me.

"Penny for your thoughts, Mr. Ogden."

"I think at this point you might as well call me Wayne."

"Oh, no, if I do then I'll slip up and call you that at work, and then everybody will know. Trust me, it's happened before."

"You've done this sort of thing, then, before?"

"Never at Collins, but at my last job. I had to. My gosh, even when Mr. Caspian's home he barely gives me what I need."

"You think he messes around on the road?"

"I think he doesn't like sex is what I think."

I tried to imagine what that would be like and failed. "If you're Catholic, what do people think about your not having any kids?"

"They think we're among those poor unfortunates that the Lord made barren, and they pray for a miracle." She raised her left foot off the bed and wiggled her toes. "You know, Mr. Ogden, I'd say until this afternoon our department was the least scandalous in the whole company."

"How's that?"

"It's all men, except me, and none of those fellows like me that way. But just look at the rest of the place. Mr. Collins himself getting that girl in trouble and sending her away to have it gotten rid of."

"How did you find out about that?"

"I'm real nosey, Mr. Ogden. And people think I don't listen so they say things when I'm around. But I do listen."

Mrs. Caspian spent the next half hour regaling me with the misdeeds and peccadilloes of upper and middle management. If half of it was true, which I doubted, then our little aircraft manufacturing concern was a cesspool of vice and iniquity unrivaled since Nero's Rome. When I asked her about our esteemed comptroller Mr. Huff she regretted having nothing to give me. "Because he's really the one who's got it in for you and Mr. Collins. Nobody has anything bad to say about him, though. He's a big shot in the K of C and he's on all those charity boards and my gosh, have you ever seen his family?"

"I never have."

"Four of the best looking kids you ever saw. And when he was in the hospital he got over three hundred get-well cards."

"Appendectomy or something serious?"

"He was attacked and beaten up pretty bad."

I sat up. "How's that?"

"Oh, it was during the war. He was out for a walk and some hoodlums jumped him."

"You don't say. In broad daylight?"

"Oh, no, it was at night."

"And I suppose it was on a downtown sidewalk."

"No, he was walking in Riverside Park. Past midnight, I think. He said he does it sometimes to clear his head. Why are you smiling like that?" she asked.

"Mrs. Caspian, you're okay in my book."

"Thank you, Mr. Ogden," she said, and she took my hand and guided it below her belly again and gave me the kind of smile only a straying member of the cathedral choir can give.

HIRAM FISH NO longer worked for Mrs. Collins, he informed me over the phone, having fallen out with the old virago over the reimbursement of his medical expenses. He wanted me to know that there were no hard feelings and that he was available for any sort of work Mr. Collins might wish to have him undertake, including but not limited to surveillance and surreptitious photography.

"What kind of camera do you use for that kind of work?"

He cleared his throat and I remembered the Speed Graphic I'd bat-ted off the hood of his car. "It depends upon the situation," he said.

"Suppose I want to take a picture at night without the subject knowing he's been photographed?"

"Gosh, I sure don't know. I always use a bulb at night, and they sure know after that goes off."

"You think you could figure out a way? We might have some work for you if you can."

"I'd be most happy to look into it," he said, sounding like the preening gigolo he strove so hard to resemble.

I WOKE THE next morning with a toothache. It was a right rear molar and it'd been bothering me off and on for a month or more, and now it hurt so bad I was afraid I might need a root canal or worse, an extraction. I thought about going to see Dr. Werner, our old family dentist, but I remembered in him what I now recognized as a sadistic streak—he was a skimper on the Novocain, and he used to sneer when-ever a young patient cried out. He was born in the old country, and would have made a great Nazi in the movies. I didn't want to pay out the nose, either, so I headed over to the VA hospital on Kellogg and waited for an hour with half a dozen other guys until my name was finally called.

The ex-army dentist who examined me lectured me on the evils of sweets and the importance of good dental hygiene before putting the gas mask on me and drilling away at what was still, in his estimation, a manageable cavity. Dr. Werner hadn't approved of the laughing gas, as he thought it might lead to narcotic use, and I saw now that the old Kraut had a point; if I wasn't literally laughing I sure felt like it.

There was a sense of separation from my body, as well as a sense that I was doing cartwheels while still seated and immobile in the torture chair, and I made a mental note never to start using Hycodan myself, a thought that came a half-second after the thought that maybe it would be worth trying out some of the old man's pills. No, thanks, I'll stick to peddling the stuff.

I was walking through the atrium, mouth full of gauze, when I ran into Bunk Fletcher, a kid I'd grown up with and hadn't seen since I was inducted.

He was out of the army and working for the VA as a file clerk. Despite my temporary speech impediment, we fell to talking and he invited me up to his office to jaw and drink Uncle Sam's watery coffee.

He was showing me the filing system and I asked him, just for laughs, to pull my file. He did it, and I was impressed with its thoroughness and accuracy. My whole military career, at least the comings and goings, and all the pertinent medical data were there, along with an identification photo that may have been the dourest image of me ever captured on film. All my transfers, from Fort Dix all the way to Rome and finally my discharge, were right on there. My current address, as well as my last one, were in there, too, as well as the fact that I worked at Collins, even in which department. It got me thinking how easy it would be for the military to find me if for some reason I wanted to drop off the face of the earth.

"This the only copy?" I asked Bunk.

"There's one on file in Washington, updated from your local file."

"What if someone wanted to see it?"

"They'd have to have a pretty good reason. We keep a pretty tight lid on these things."

A real tight army lid, he meant, and I knew better than anybody how easy those were to pry off. If you knew how.

SALLY SURPRISED ME when I came in that night with a houseful of new furniture from Bellow's. The front half of the parlor contained an oak dining room set, with a credenza along the wall. In the rear half, which she now insisted on calling the living room, sat a new davenport and, to my horror, an overstuffed fauteuil that had replaced my father's old reading chair.

My father was a genial and quiet man who had a life of the mind quite separate from his daily mathematical routine, an important corrective against seeing life as a ledger. When I enrolled in Wichita University my father urged me to study business, a subject that interested me not at all; by the time I was in the army selling tires and gasoline and running whores, though, I was immensely grateful to him for the advice. He read every night in that chair, and on nights when I was home so did I. I was not happy to see it gone.

My silence had put a scare into her, and her voice was very quiet when she asked me how I liked it. Typically, she hadn't run through in her mind all the possible reactions to her expensive little surprise. I didn't want to be an ogre, but I couldn't pretend to be happy about it.

"How much?"

"A little less than a thousand, in installments. It was a bargain, if you look at what these pieces all cost individually. And they gave us a special extra five percent discount, with you being a vet and all."

"Where's the old furniture?"

"They took it away."

"And did you get a trade-in? A discount for the value of the old furniture?"

"I didn't think to ask."

I walked out without another word.

I FOUND THE manager standing in the back of the furniture store selling a bedstead to a young couple who looked as though they were saving it for the wedding night. The boy's eyes looked like they were going to pop right out of his skull if he didn't dip his wick pretty soon, which was understandable given the healthy young specimen of femininity at his side. I'd made it clear to the other clerks that the manager was the only one I'd do business with, and I must have looked serious because they kept their distance. The manager was getting flustered, and finally he met my steady glare.

"Can one, ah, one of our salesmen help you, sir?"

"You're the manager, you're the one I need to see. I'll wait."

"Is this about an adjustment?"

"You might say that." I made a point of keeping my voice low; nothing betrays weakness like an emotional outburst. "Your boys cheated my wife in my absence, and I'm here to see it set right."

The young couple exchanged glances.

"I'm sure if there's been some kind of misunderstanding one of the salesmen can help, they're authorized . . . "

"I'll wait. You sell the lovebirds their nuptial bed and we'll talk afterward."

"Actually we're going to wait a day or two and think about it," the boy said, and the girl whacked his elbow.

"I want to get it now, Herbie," she hissed as Herbie pulled her away by the arm.

"Sorry if I cost you a sale," I said, without the least trace of sorrow in my voice.

"That's quite all right, couples often need to ponder a major purchase, especially just starting out. Now what was the problem with your wife?"

"It's not a problem with my wife, it's a problem with your sales force. They had a whole houseful of perfectly good furniture hauled out of my place this afternoon with no credit given in return."

"Of course we're dealers in new furniture only."

"I don't give a damn, you know perfectly well you don't give good material away to the Salvation Army. You sell them someplace, now I want some of those pieces back, and I want compensation for the rest."

"As far as I'm concerned, sir, you're not entitled to any. If your wife had mentioned compensation at the time we would have informed her . . . "

"Listen to me. What's your name?"

"Stan Franklin."

"All right, Stan, I notice Bellows has an ad once a week in the *Eagle* but not the *Beacon*. Old man Bellows got something against the Jews?"

"Mr. Bellows happens to be my father-in-law, and he doesn't feel that the *Beacon*'s readers are our type of clientele."

"I mention it because I know the *Eagle* wouldn't run a story about a naïve mother-to-be, the wife of a vet, getting gypped by one of their own advertisers, but I bet the *Beacon* would jump at it. Of course, that wouldn't matter to you, since none of your customers read the *Beacon*."

TWO HUNDRED DOLLARS off the price of the furniture, and my dad's old chair would be delivered in the morning. I was a little disappointed that old Bellows caved in so quickly when his son-in-law phoned him. What I'd really wanted was to smash one of their expensive tables to pieces and beat Mr. Stan Franklin to a bleeding pulp with one of its legs, after which I might allow the remainder of the sales force to flee before I soaked the place in kerosene and watched it burn to the ground. Maybe, I thought, I needed a drink.

THREE SOAKS, TWO men and a woman, were swozzled over at Norman's blind pig. Norman introduced them but their names wouldn't stick in my head so I ended up calling the woman Honey, the taller of the two men Stretch, and the fatter one Tub. Neither of the men seemed to like his nickname much, but neither said anything at first. The woman warmed to hers, spilling out of her girdle with her eyes at half mast, mascara running with sweat and possibly tears from earlier in the evening.

Tub and Stretch were vying for her favors, and my arrival had made them question the short-term wisdom of that rivalry. The presence of an interloper called for a united front, lest Honey decide against both of them. Norman was a friend, so I let the rubes' veiled insults roll off my back at first.

Later, though, an innocent mention of my war record on Norman's part set Stretch off on a long, rolling diatribe about returning servicemen and the easy ride we had. When I didn't challenge his assertions he got madder and started dropping hints that I might have fabricated my service record. I didn't really give a good goddamn what these idiots thought about me, but the bourbon was starting to make me feel mean.

"You may be right, Stretch. You know my wife got a whole five percent off a dining room suite this afternoon, just by virtue of me having been overseas? Shit, if I'd know about the five percent veteran's discount at Bellow's Furniture Emporium I'd have signed up before Pearl Harbor."

Stretch made a face like someone had just cut a fart, and he looked away from all of us, sniffling in distaste.

"Don't worry about it," I said. "Lots of guys got classed 4-F. Nobody thinks the worse of you for it."

"Who says I was 4-F?"

"Fallen arches, maybe?"

"I'll be damned if it's any of your business. Just maybe I was essential personnel."

"Say, folks, how about a round on the house?" Norman said.

"What's your line, Tub?" I asked, trying to salvage the situation.

"I'm an assistant mortician," he said. I felt a little pity at the thought of him draining the blood out of bodies into a little floor drain in the center of a dark, antiseptic room. I wanted him to get Honey's favors for the night, to know the touch of a living woman's hand for a change.

"That's interesting work. I was in the Quartermaster Corps; we used to furnish the army morticians with all their gear." I looked at Honey. "It's more complicated work than you might imagine."

Stretch squirmed in his chair. "That's no way for a man to make a living, touching corpses. What kind of woman would want your hands on her knowing where they've been?"

"What do you do, Stretch?"

"I," he said with a drunk's exaggerated, pious dignity, "am an insurance adjuster."

"So your racket is cheating people out of money they're legitimately due at the lowest points of their lives."

Stretch rose to his wobbly feet and, teetering, grabbed the back of the chair for support. "That's a damnable lie, sir. I make sure cheats aren't soaking the insurance company, and I keep everybody's rates low. That's what I do, sir."

"You're a jackal," I said, and at that he took a swing at me. I stood and dodged it and gave him the bum's rush to the stairs. Behind me Honey let out an incredulous whoop as I kicked Stretch in the pants. He tumbled headlong down the staircase and hit his head hard on the door, cracking one of its glass panes. He turned, thrashing, but I had the door open before he could get his feet planted, and when he hit the gravel I gave him a swift kick to the belly while upstairs Honey cackled with delight. He vomited, narrowly missing my shoe.

"Now take a fucking hike before I crack your skull wide open," I said as I headed back upstairs.

THE ADRENALINE HAD burned off some of the alcohol, and I had Norman pour me another bourbon. The violence had flushed some toxin out of my system and I felt good, really good, for the first time in days. Tub and Honey, his hand up her skirt provoking a heady giggle, seemed to have forgotten about me. They finished their drinks and got ready to leave.

"Mister," Honey said at the top of the stairs, her hair and makeup wrecked, "you sure gave old Nate what for."

Norman busied himself with KP and I apologized for kicking Stretch down the stairs.

"That's all right, I get tired of listening to that son of a bitch anyway."

"I guess Tub's going to get himself some tail tonight."

"You think so?" Norman seemed surprised.

"Are you shitting me? Those two horndogs were about to come to blows over the old floozy."

"Huh. 'Cause she's married to Nate, the fellow you kicked down the stairs." He got the bottle and poured me another, then sat down and grimaced. "My hip. Hurts like a son of a bitch and the doc says there's nothing to be done."

"You ought to try some Hycodan. Only problem is you can't take a shit or pop a hard on."

"I think I'll stay away from that, thanks. I knew some hypos when I was young and it never went too well."

"You don't have to shoot it up, it comes in a pill."

"Still and all. One of my few pleasures left in life is my morning dump. And if some dame came in here and wanted me to jump her I'd like to leave the possibility open."

"Hell, get yourself a whore."

"I'm not comfortable with the idea of paying for it. Last time I did that I caught myself a hell of a dose."

After lecturing Norman about the proper relationship between rubbers and harlotry I sat contemplating my glass, feeling the warm elation of the evening's violence dissipate, replaced by a dull, empty aching. The worst part was the realization that the ache was one I'd been feeling for weeks or months without ever noticing it. "Did you ever want to kill someone?"

"Sure," he said. "Lots of times."

"Ever think about really doing it?"

I BID NORMAN good night and drove home woozy. I walked into the house ready to report to Sally the happy outcome of her misadventure at Bellows Furnishings, but it was one-fifteen in the morning and she had gone to bed long before. That was a shame, because I wasn't mad at her anymore. The new dining room table was still set for dinner for two, which made me think for the first time that evening that I hadn't eaten since lunchtime. I opened the icebox and found two steaks on a plate.

Though my domestic skills were few, I could fry a steak. I got out a cast iron skillet, the same one Sally had tried to brain me with, and melted a couple of pats of butter. When that started sizzling I dropped the larger of the steaks into the skillet and while it was still good and rare slapped it onto a plate and ate it at the head of the dining room table. The wooziness had begun to dissipate by the time I finished, and I crept down the hallway to the bedroom. There I was surprised by lamplight and a neatly made bed. "Sally?" I called out, knowing that it was pointless; she was off somewhere, teaching me a lesson. I undressed and went to bed, and despite my late meal and the unaccustomed amount of bourbon in my belly I slept soundly and without dreams.

ELEVEN
FATHER FLANAGAN
CONTRADICTS HIMSELF

THE NEXT LETTER was postmarked St. Louis and read:

*What kind of man cheats the govement hes' fighting for in
the first place? You have got no shame or humility and you
caused heartbeaks. Ill be heading your way soon and youll
be none the wiser as to when.*

This time he included a lock of black hair, one I assumed belonged
to one of my Roman girls and not to the sender himself. I was momentarily at a loss as to how to proceed, and all this was irritating the hell
out of me, given all the other grief I was being handed at the moment.

THE MATTER OF Mr. Huff was still on the agenda. Park was concerned about getting ourselves or the boss implicated if he or I did
anything illegal or untoward, so I phoned Hiram Fish at his office and
arranged to meet him for chop suey at the Bellflower Café downtown.

He flinched a little when he saw me walk in the door but had mastered himself admirably by the time I sat down at his booth.

The chop suey tasted like shit, but at the Bellflower that was a tradition and I wouldn't have wanted it any different. "How come you suppose they serve Chinese food in a place with nary a sole Chinaman on the premises?" he asked.

"Bellflower used to buy scraps from the butchers and fry it up every which way, and calling it chop suey kept people from wondering much what they were eating."

"I had real Chinese food in San Francisco when I was in the Merchant Marines," he said. "Wasn't like this at all. San Francisco, there's a wide open town, drunks and whores and hopheads all over the place. Hell, I may head out there again. Now that the war's done there's plenty of opportunity for a man like me."

He was talking fast and nervous, one of those people who's afraid in an awkward situation that a few moments' silence will reveal something terrible, so I let him babble for a while until he let drop something that made me understand why he was so nervous: He thought we wanted him to spy on old Mrs. Collins.

"I suppose you're going to tell me she gave a whole troop of Boy Scouts the clap."

He looked blank for a second. "I don't know what she did. Usually it's wives want husbands watched or vicey-versey, so I thought Mr. Collins might want me to keep an eye on her."

"Hell, let her go to her DAR meetings, Collins doesn't give a damn what she does."

"What, then?"

"I want you to get a picture of a guy with a dick in his mouth."

Again the blank look, followed by a troubled squint. "You mean like via mail order?"

I almost got up and left right there; either he was playing at being obtuse or he was a genuinely stupid son of a bitch. "I need you to follow a particular fellow who means Mr. Collins harm. I have reason to believe this fellow gets his pleasure in Riverside Park late at night, and I want you to sneak up on him in flagrante delicto . . . "

"In where?"

"In the middle of sucking a dick."

"Who is this guy?"

I handed him a manila envelope, which he started to open right there, the dumb shit. "Open it later, damn it. His picture's in there and his address and everything I have on him."

"I'll get on it this afternoon. It'll take me a week or so to establish his habits, get to know his comings and goings, that's at twenty a day, with a fifty dollar deposit."

"Don't hand me that crap, Hiram. This is worth five hundred, but only if you get us a crystal clear picture of the guy on his knees with a pair of balls bouncing off his chin. Until that picture's in our hands you get doodly squat."

"If that's the way you feel . . . " He started to rise, and when I didn't try to stop him he sat down again. "Listen, I got expenses. How about twenty to tide me over?"

I handed him the ten I'd been planning to all along, and spent the rest of my lunch half-listening to the cascade of ill fortune he'd been subject to over the last few months.

"It's because you're a fink," I said.

"What?"

"No offense. But you're in a profession that calls for you to be a fink, and no good fortune is going to come your way until you repent."

He nodded, expression blank again, and seemed to be reflecting on the surprising news that he was a professional rat. I was glad to have enlightened him, and when it was time to go I magnanimously paid the check and left a princely half dollar on the table for our stick insect of a waitress.

A WEEK LATER Hiram Fish left a message with Mrs. Caspian for me to meet him at his office on North Broadway. It was down a narrow, dark corridor above a camera shop, and he gave a start when I opened the door without knocking. His skittishness was understandable; both eyes were purple and black and his discolored nose was a few degrees off true. A grisly line of stitches ran horizontally beneath his mouth, and his left arm was in a sling. Two of the fingers on his right hand were in splints.

"Sweet Baby Jesus, Fish, what the hell happened to you?"

"I was tailing your man Huff all week. Home, the plant, home, the plant, nothing. Then Friday night he leaves the car parked in the driveway instead of inside the garage. Around eleven-thirty he leaves the house, rolls the car down into the street without turning the engine over. Gets her a little momentum and turns it over real quiet, did a good job. You can bet he'd done that before."

"Wouldn't surprise me."

"There's hardly any traffic so I can't just pull out and follow without him noticing. But I remember what you said about Riverside Park, so I waited until he was out of sight and headed on over there via Douglas instead of Central, which is the way he was headed."

He was clearly proud of his initiative and creative thinking, but not wanting to give him a swelled head I said nothing.

"So I get to Riverside Park and I get out with the Speed Graphic and snuck around for a while trying to find him. Well, guess what? That goddamn park is chock full of queers, and one of 'em spots me and the camera. Says 'What's the big idea?' And I didn't even think this guy was queer, more like your linebacker type. I didn't know what the hell he'd be doing there that time of night, but I told him I was there to get a picture. 'Picture of what?' the linebacker says. 'You wouldn't believe it,' I tell him, 'but all these guys walking around? They're fairies. One of 'em's gonna get his picture taken sucking a dick.' Well what do you know, the guy calls over somebody else, and that guy calls over somebody else, and pretty soon there's a whole bunch of fairies giving me shit about wanting to take the picture. Then one of 'em hits me, and then another one takes the Speed Graphic and smashes the shit out of it. Pretty soon the linebacker's kicking the hell out of me, and about the third kick to my ribs I figure out he's one of 'em. Can you beat that? Hell, half of 'em just looked like regular guys. And even the little ones were punching me pretty hard."

I gave him my best deadpan stare and waited a long moment before responding. "Then I'm assuming you don't have the picture."

"I just told you they smashed the camera! That's the second one I've lost this year, you might recall."

My expression didn't change, which was difficult because I really wanted to laugh at the poor dumb shit. "If you don't have my picture, why did you call me down here?"

"Well, tell you the truth, I was kind of hoping you'd pay my expenses on this. Replace the camera, pay my medical bills."

"You're a moron. You stroll casually into a well-known queer hangout, full of guys with a big goddamn secret, carrying the camera under your arm? And without knowing exactly where the mark is, just looking around for him? Are you kidding me? What did you intend to do when you found him? Ask him if he can say 'cheese' with his mouth full?"

Fish cleared his throat and winced. I was pretty sure he had the idea by now that the interview wasn't going well. "I'd sure like help with my doctor bill. I ended up driving over to St. Francis with one eye swollen clear shut and the other barely open. I still hurt something awful."

"Not a chance."

"If you'll recall, I quit working for Mrs. Collins over a medical bill."

"I recall, all right."

"And I came to you offering to watch her for Mr. Collins." Despite the attempt at a threat there was still a pleading overtone to his thin, nasal voice.

"If you're implying that you'd ever go work for Huff against the old man I can tell you right now I'd gut you like a fucking catfish. Then again, considering what a king fuck-up you are, maybe I should call Huff and recommend you."

"How about replacing the camera, at least? How can I take that picture without a camera?"

"I don't want you to take it. You're lucky I don't take the ten spot back. For all we know Huff may be onto us now."

"I never said his name, I just said I was looking for a guy."

"Maybe not, but you can be sure the queer network has got the word around town you were looking to snap someone. They have to protect their own, you dumb shit."

"So what's the next move?"

"For you? There isn't one. Wait around for the phone to ring."

"I'm fired?"

"That's right."

"You mean all that and I'm out of pocket on this job?"

"That's right. And quit looking at me like a whipped pup. Count yourself lucky no one decided to fuck you, pretty boy that you were up 'til Friday night."

I WENT DOWNSTAIRS to the camera store and looked at what was available. The larger formats like Fish's Speed Graphic were expensive and bulky, but there were a number of smaller cameras that might fit the bill. I settled on a German 35 millimeter model with a reasonably fast lens and bought four rolls of the fastest black and white film Kodak made. I added to the sale a used printer and the makings of a basic darkroom and hauled the crateful of equipment out to the Olds. In the morning I'd present Miss Grau with my receipts; in the meantime I was going home to set up a darkroom in the basement and take a few practice rolls.

"MY DONALD WANTS to meet you," Millie Grau said the next morning while she was filling out the form for my reimbursement.

"He does?" I said, feeling some mild alarm.

"He thinks what you're doing for Mr. Collins is wonderful. And I should add that I do too."

"Oh," I said. I wondered if they were thinking of my procuring whores for the boss, or getting him hooked on narcotics, or maybe it was the blackmailing business.

Miss Grau was blushing, something she did with great charm, spontaneously and fairly often. "You know I would never say this to most people, but Mrs. Collins is really a nasty old . . . " She groped for the right word for a moment and blushed a little deeper. "Old hag."

"How's that?"

"She calls me and says the most terrible lies about Mr. Collins. Horrible things."

"What sorts of things?"

"She told me about that girl Emily, you know the one."

"Sure."

"Well I knew all about it, but I wasn't going to acknowledge anything of the sort to her. And you know what? I think she got a great big kick out of telling me. Trying to shock me. Make me hate him."

You should hate him, I thought, but one of her most appealing traits was that blind loyalty.

"And the things she said about the girl, the things she called her." Millie was starting to break down, the blush covering her throat as well as her face, her eyes wet but not yet dripping. "You know that could happen to just about any girl," she said, and grasped blindly for a Kleenex from the dispenser on her desk. I plucked one and applied it to her eyes. "Can I tell you something, Mr. Ogden?"

"Sure."

"You can't tell anyone, ever."

"You have my word."

"I really like you, in fact you're the only person here besides Mr. Collins I think of as . . . as a friend, if you see what I mean."

"Sure," I said. We were both sitting now, my chair pulled close to her desk.

"Before I came here, I was engaged to a boy in Wisconsin."

"I didn't know you were from Wisconsin."

"Uh-huh. Anyway, there was this boy, and we were engaged, and he . . . he took off one day. Said he was joining the army—this was in '42, everybody was joining up. Well, guess what I found out? I was . . . " She looked me in the eye, as though second-guessing her previous judgment as to my trustworthiness. Apparently I passed, because the next thing she said bowled me over. "I found out I was pregnant."

I'd assumed Miss Millie Grau's hymen was intact and under lock and key; the news that she was a retread virgin, called back to righteousness by some misguided impulse, shook me. The poor kid, I thought.

"You think that's terrible?"

"Not at all. That's life. So what about the fiancé?"

"That's the next thing I found out. I tried to contact him through the army, and they said there was no such recruit. I checked the navy, too, and finally I went to the recruiting office in Fond du Lac, and I found out he was 4-F. He'd just skipped out."

"You poor kid."

"So I went to one of those homes for unwed mothers, this place in Michigan where nobody knew me, and I had the baby there. He was adopted by some nice family and that was that. But you know, I think about him every day.

"Anyway, that's how I ended up in Wichita. I couldn't go back to my folks'. And you and Mr. Collins are the only people I've ever told it to since I got here. I guess one reason I got so upset just then was I haven't told Donald."

"You think he might react badly?"

"He's a minister."

"Then he's heard a thousand times worse."

"Sure, but not from the girl he's going to marry. He thinks I'm a, you know."

"Right. Well, don't tell him."

"But then it's like a lie."

"It's an omission."

She stood up. "What you must think of me, Mr. Ogden."

"Same as always, Millie, the world." I dared then to reach out and squeeze her shoulder pad and then, giving her a broad, friendly, avuncular smile, left her office.

THE NIGHT SHOTS I took were inadequate, even when I pushed the exposure by two stops, which ruined the contrast anyway. I was about to abandon the whole project when I realized that the tiny metal socket on the front of the camera's body was intended for a flash attachment. Once I'd bought such a device plus a couple of dozen bulbs and bolted it to the side of the camera I found I had all I needed. The first night I got a shot of a hissing mother opossum in the back yard, its primeval marsupial fangs bared at the loping biped violating her territory. The picture came out so nicely I made an eight by ten enlargement and got a frame for it the next morning on the way in to work, then hung the thing on the wall behind my desk.

I had a tactical problem, though, now that I had solved the technical one. As far as I knew, all of Mr. Huff's fellating was performed in the wee hours of the morning in the company of his fellows; the firing of flash gun would inevitably attract the unwelcome attention of the park's other denizens, and in all likelihood I'd end up getting the same treatment as Fish, the camera wrecked and the film inside ruined.

IN THE CAFETERIA I was spotted by Mr. Rackey, who boldly joined me. I almost never ate lunch at the plant, but I'd arrived and hung my picture at eleven-thirty and it didn't seem worth the trouble driving off the premises.

"Do you know what I did once?" he asked me.

"I sure don't," I said.

"Set a barn on fire when I was sixteen, this old son of a bitch was yelling at me and my buddies, saying I thought I told you kids to get off my goddamn property. You ever hear of Boy's Town? Judge sent me there. Didn't do me a lick of good. You know how old Father Flanagan's supposed to have said 'there's no such thing as a bad boy?' That was before the old bastard met me."

"Never knew anyone who went to Boy's Town before."

"It wasn't so bad. Beats any other kind of lockup I was ever in. Hey, Ogden, you been back to Red's lately?"

"It's been a little while."

"I got eighty-sixed last week, forever."

"What for?" I couldn't remember too many people being eighty-sixed from Red's, even temporarily, so Rackey's transgression must have been serious.

"Broke that whore's arm."

"Which whore is that?"

"Hell, I don't know all their names. Kind of flabby but not too hard to look at."

"Barbara?"

"That's it. Barbara."

"That skinny bartender with the bushy eyebrows has it for her pretty bad. How'd you end up breaking her arm?"

"She wouldn't dance with me, wouldn't even get up off her moneymaker, so I yanked her out of the chair and bent her arm right back."

He grinned, his mouth a spectacle of jagged, multicolored teeth, proud of himself and his prowess with the ladies.

THAT AFTERNOON I found Millie Grau a distracted wreck, pulling nervously at a loose strand of hair at her temple and looking like she'd missed a couple of nights' worth of sleep.

"I told him, Mr. Ogden. He's broken it off temporarily while he prays on it. He . . . he says he feels like he doesn't really know me any more. Like . . . like I was lying to him all along."

"Sorry, Millie," I said.

"I was, wasn't I? Lying?"

"No, you weren't, and if he's any kind of a man he'll put this behind him."

I left her feeling a little better, I thought. I didn't know what the matter was with this two-bit tent preacher anyway, but if he let Millie Grau get away because he wasn't the first one in, that made him a stupid shit in my book.

That night Sally fixed a casserole, the recipe for which she'd found in one of the numerous ladies' magazines to which she now subscribed. It was awful, a grisly olio of mayonnaise, cheap canned tuna, and a variety of cheese I'd never encountered before that possessed an unsettling metallic undertaste. I ate a large portion and pretended to be pleased, and afterward when I suggested a detour to the bedroom before she washed the dishes she demurred.

"I'm just not feeling that way tonight," she said.

"That's fine," I said.

A few months earlier I might have cursed Sally to her face and given her a hard time for her reluctance to perform her marital chore. Now was a different story; now I understood that a noxious potage of baby chemicals was making her temporarily crazy. I kissed her and said it was all right, and would she mind if I went out to meet some friends for a beer?

All my friends were in the army, though, so instead I headed for the Eaton hotel, got Herman Nester on the phone, and asked for a girl to be sent up.

"Any one in particular, or should I surprise you?" he said.

"Is Irma available?" I hadn't ever requested a specific girl before, but the memory of her lingered pleasantly.

When Irma showed up she put her hands on her hips and said, "Well look who it is. The ass man."

"Not tonight, I don't think."

"Good, 'cause the pounding you gave me last time kept me on my feet for a week."

It was standard whore flattery, but she was nice to bother with it. "You want a drink?"

"Sure," she said, "bourbon if you got it."

I poured her a drink. She had her hair done differently, swept up instead of bangs the way she wore it last time, and though she was arguably prettier this way she no longer bore such a striking resemblance to Joan Blondell. I didn't care much, as long as all of her parts functioned.

"So where's the old guy tonight?"

"Don't know. He doesn't get around like as he used to."

"He some kind of hypo? Was that the problem last time?"

"Something like that."

"Yeah, that's what I guessed. I was married to one for a while. After a while it's fine with him if he can't get it up, 'cause he doesn't even want to. Why fuck when you could be fixing?"

"He doesn't fix. The old man's hooked on pills."

"Heroin pills? I never heard of that."

"Not heroin. Something like it."

"Huh." She downed her drink and rattled the ice cubes, swirling them around faster and faster at the bottom of the glass. "What do you feel like tonight?" she asked.

HALF AN HOUR later she was taking a shower while I lay there on the bed, thinking I should have brought that little 35 millimeter camera with me. The thought triggered a snicker; what the hell would I do with naked arty farty pictures of Irma? Jerk off to them? Sell them through Merle Tessler's outfit in KC? No, it wasn't my kind of thing. I was no Edward Weston, no Albert Stieglitz. I was born to sell pornography, not create it.

When Irma came out of the bathroom, though, still toweling her torso dry, skin still pink from the hot water, a curious natural grace to the sway of her hips as she crossed the room from bathroom to bed and hopped on, I had second thoughts. I'd pay for pictures of that.

"You're paid up for another hour," she said. "Just in case you might want another turn."

"I will in a little bit."

I lay there for a little while staring at the ceiling, thinking about nothing and content to do so. She startled me out of my trance by asking me if something was eating me.

"What makes you say that?"

"You look like something's on your mind, that's all. Sometimes guys'll hire a gal just to talk about stuff they can't tell wifey or their pals."

This wasn't news to me. In Italy, fully a quarter of our trade was guys who just wanted a sympathetic female ear, which was fine with me as long as the hour was paid up. On a whim I sketched out my difficulties with Huff, without naming any names, and she listened attentively.

"You ought to stake out one of the queer bars," she said when I was finished.

"I didn't know there were any."

"Sure, they're just like any other bars except full of homos."

"I know what they are, I just meant I didn't know there were any in Wichita."

"Sure, where do you think they hang around?"

"You know a lot about queers," I said.

"I know a few. I didn't tell you this, but there's two that work for Nester."

"Nester's pimping men?" I didn't think I was easy to shock, but that one came clear out of left field.

"Keep that under your hat." She propped up her right knee and picked at the bright red nail of her little toe.

"What do you think about baby names?" Sally asked me a couple of days hence over a breakfast of ruined grey eggs and carbonized bacon, washed down by coffee that was too strong, a welcome relief from her usual thin and transparent brew.

"I think they should all have one."

"I'm perfectly serious."

"All right, if it's a boy we name it after my father or my grandfather. If it's a girl I don't care."

"If it's a girl I was thinking about either Linda or Loretta," she said.

People were always telling Sally she looked like one movie star or another, and the two most frequently named were Linda Darnell and Loretta Young. I wasn't kidding when I said I didn't care what it was named, though. "Either one's fine with me."

I had a little break regarding that other pain in my ass at the moment, my pen pal, in the form of another envelope postmarked St. Louis. This letter consisted of only a single line:

The wages of sin is death and you are about big of one as I ever.

But this time he included a photograph of a certain Brunela, confirming my theory that he was a former GI client from Rome. I tried to remember her last name—Castelli? Cantelli?—but failed. It was a glum, head-on shot that might have been attached to an identification card. Maybe it was a mug shot, though that would have been trickier for my correspondent to get his hands on. Brunela was surly, chronically drunk, and she was one of three in my stable who'd died during my time in Italy. She swallowed poison, which could hardly be lain at my door, but who knows how the mind of a lunatic works. In any case this fellow blamed me for Brunela's death, and my job now was to rack my brain and try to remember who, if any, her special devotees were.

IRMA HAD PROMISED me she'd talk to one of the male whores in Nester's employ about getting a snap of Huff in a compromising position. I was turning over in my head ways that might work and coming up short every time. I would probably have to teach one of them to use the camera, but who knew if he'd be good enough to get the shot and make it printable? We couldn't afford another mistake like Hiram Fish.

Nester set up a meet with one of them, and Park and I sat in a booth at the Bellflower and were joined by an unexceptional looking man of about thirty.

"Brad Wageknecht. Something about some pictures you needed taken?"

Park was giving him the once-over, deep curiosity in his face. I filled Wageknecht in on our progress so far and he nodded, his eyes closed.

"First of all, a four-by-five's too big for that kind of work," he said. "Even 35 millimeter's going to be spotted. What you want is a spy camera. Ever hear of a thing called a Minox?"

"No."

"Brought one back from Germany. Spy camera, uses a tiny little film cartridge. Great pictures, you know, Swiss lenses. It would have to be indoors, at a party or a bar, though, since I don't have any way to attach a bulb to it."

Park was practically dancing in his chair. "You were in the war? Germany?"

"The Big Red One," Wageknecht said.

"Fuck you, that's not true."

He opened his shirt, an action that drew a flinch from Park, and revealed a scar twice as long and thick as the one on my own chest. "Doesn't matter anyway," he said. "I got nothing left to prove."

I gave him a hundred dollar advance and the promise of four hundred more for a picture that met our requirements, and he left.

As we prepared to leave Park was very quiet, and he didn't speak until we were in the parking lot.

"Not a chance in hell he's queer. Hell, he's a goddamn war hero."

"I imagine a few of them were, Herman."

"The hell you say." He shook his head, a little angrily, as though he was going to have to go through his whole company in his head now and wonder which ones were and which weren't.

TWELVE

CLYDE BEATTY'S
PRIZE ORANG-OUTANG

THE NEXT ANONYMOUS letter arrived at the house, which actually gave me a little scare. It was one thing to know where I worked, but he'd found out awfully fast that I'd moved. It read:

> *You know whose going to be real interseted in that money*
> *of yours is the fBi old J Egdar will get a big laugh out of*
> *watching you hung out to dry*

Also enclosed was a copy print of a more flattering picture of Brunella, in which she smiled endearingly at the photographer—was he my unnamed tormentor?—while brushing her hair over her left ear. I'd come up with a few of her paying admirers in my mind, but I was damned if I had names for any of them. I thought of them as a blur of barely distinguishing features: the balding one, the wall-eyed one, the walking Adam's apple, the drooler.

Whoever he was he seemed to be having trouble making up his mind as to whether he was going to kill me or turn me in or fuck my wife. This one was postmarked St. Louis like the last two, and I wondered what his business was there, and when he'd be done with it.

A BOARD MEETING scheduled for later in the month seemed a logical time for the conspirators to launch an attack on the old man, whose normal short-tempered demeanor had been replaced by a glassy, demented calm, whose permanence was punctuated by rages more severe and without apparent cause than usual. We needed him off the Hycodan, at least temporarily.

I met Park for lunch at Stanley's. It was two PM, so most of the lunch crowd was gone by the time we sat down. "How's the boss the last couple of days?"

"Worse. You know how for a while he was okay while he was dosed? Any more he's either hurting for it or he's a sleepwalker. Thirty of the damned things a day. Costing a fortune, not that that bothers him."

"Are we agreed, then, that we need to get him off it?"

"I guess so. I don't think it's going to be easy."

"I don't guess it is, but I've got an idea. You ever been to Hot Springs?"

"Down in Arkansas? Nope."

"I talked to a man at the Arlington Hotel about a suite. Place's got an interior bedroom that's practically soundproofed so he can yell all he wants."

"How come you can't take somebody else along? What about that crazy man you got a job down on the floor?"

"You're the driver, Park. We can't take the train, God only knows what kind of messes he'd get into in public. And you're the bodyguard, too, don't forget."

"I don't know. What if he dies? I think they do sometimes, coming down off morphine."

"It's not morphine, Park, you know that."

He was eating a grilled cheese sandwich, picking at the fries that came with it and dunking them in his coffee, a habit I found so distracting that I wouldn't have hired him had he tried it during our first interview.

"Whatever you call it, we better talk to that doctor before he tries kicking it."

PARK WAS RIGHT. A couple of laymen like us might have killed a man going through withdrawal, especially a man of Collins's years. I spent the afternoon finalizing the plans for the trip to Hot Springs and phoned Ezra Groff, who disapproved of the plan.

"You ought to just gradually reduce his dose," he said with some irritation at my failure to heed his advice. "I told you at the start, this stuff isn't as addictive as morphine or heroin. It's my belief that the man could get down to a reasonable daily dosage and do just fine."

PARK POINTED OUT to me that a departure from Collins Field, or even Wichita Municipal, might spark rumors. Add to that neither one of us knew a pilot we could trust, so we started out on US 160 eastward two mornings later in the company Olds with Collins in the back seat, looking out the window at nothing and nearly catatonic. He didn't even know where we were going or why; so passive had the old geezer become in his dependence on his medicine it was enough to tell him that if he wanted his dose he'd have to go on a ride to get it.

We stopped in my Dad's hometown of Cottonwood and had a late lunch at the Jayhawk diner on Lincoln. The counterman was a chubby fellow with a shiny red face, and when he recommended the hash, Park and I ordered it. Collins refused to speak a word and got nothing, which seemed to suit him fine. I asked him if he was sure he didn't want some coffee, and he half-growled, half-muttered something unintelligible but seemingly heartfelt. When I asked him to repeat it he shouted loud and clear: "I don't drink coffee any more because it makes me want to piss and I can't. Satisfied?"

The only other customers in the diner at that hour, a pair of old ladies, laughed furtively behind their hands, and the counterman worked his toothpick around in his teeth and looked like he wasn't quite sure whether to throw us out.

"Sorry, Mister," I said. "Our Dad's a little bit confused these days."

He nodded and forgave us. "My father-in-law's getting that way."

DESPITE ANOTHER DOSE of his medicine the boss was irascible and combative on the late afternoon leg of the trip, and he went berserk when Park accidentally let slip that the purpose of the trip was the narcotics version of a drying-out cure.

"I'll be dipped in shit if I'll let my employees dictate to me when and whether I'll be taking one goddamn medicine or another! By all that's fucking holy, you will stop this vehicle right now and surrender the wheel!"

"Sorry, Mr. Collins, I can't do that," Park said.

"All right, goddamn it, I'll get a ride with somebody else," he said, and with that he grabbed the door handle and tried to exit the Olds, which at that moment was hurtling down the road at about sixty per. I reached over the seat and grabbed Collins by his arm while Park pulled over to the shoulder.

"What do we do now?" Park asked as Collins thrashed in a fruitless effort to free himself from my grasp.

"Get the trunk open."

Despite Collins's self-inflicted infirmity, getting him into the trunk wasn't easy, and once we'd closed it he kicked at the lid with a ferocity I'd rarely seen, even from him. He kept kicking as we drove on, more and more feebly as the shadows along the side of the road lengthened, and about five minutes after the kicking stopped Park turned to look at me.

"You figure there's any air getting into that trunk?" he asked.

"Probably."

"What if there isn't?"

"Then we'll make up a story and end up either in jail or looking for jobs without references."

It was late when we got in to Hot Springs, and we got the boss out of the trunk by the side of the highway before heading in to the Arlington, as pulling inert bodies out of trunks was frowned upon in your swankier establishments, even in Hot Springs. Collins was conscious but confused and cranky while I checked in, but no more so than he'd been for the last few weeks.

As I finished filling out the registration form and deposited a sizeable company check with the clerk, Collins stood closer to me than convention dictates, and said in a lucid, clear tone: "As soon as I'm off this stuff and potent again, I'm going to bang that pretty wife of yours like a goddamn gong." It didn't sound like a threat, more a well-reasoned prediction. The desk clerk, his aplomb greater than any I could have summoned at that moment, failed to display the slightest sign of having heard.

We had him booked in what I'd been told was Al Capone's favorite suite in the old days. I don't know what your average hotel suite is like in Hot Springs, but by any standards I knew Collins's was opulent to the point of immorality. One of the bedrooms was fully interior with no windows; that was Collins's room, which locked from the outside. The resort had had plenty of prior experience with dry-outs and water cures and, presumably, narco cases. Park and I had single rooms on either side of the suite, the other two rooms in the suite being reserved for the doctor and his nurse.

Doctor Hargis was recommended by the manager of the resort, Mr. Clyde Furrough, with whom I'd been frank about the reason for our stay. Doctor Hargis, the manager claimed, had gotten any number of prominent hopheads off of dope, including Errol Flynn. "He's not cheap," Furrough warned, "but he's effective and discreet."

I fell involuntarily asleep on a divan of crushed green velveteen, exhausted from the drive, the second half of which had been mine. I dreamed I was in Collins's office, choking him as he thrashed savagely, his face ladybug red and his eyes watering, tongue protruding purple and twitching, as Miss Grau and Mrs. Caspian and the rest of the secretarial pool looked on with approval and admiration.

I couldn't have been more disappointed when a brisk rapping at the door woke me promptly at nine PM. It was Doctor Hargis, accompanied by a white-haired, jowly nurse whose white orthopedic shoes squeaked with the strain every time she took a step. He explained to me my part in the procedure, which consisted entirely of paying his fee, half of it up front. I wrote him a check on Collins's personal account, which he folded neatly into quarters and put in his vest pocket. He had a pointed van dyke and round glasses that together gave him the air of an old Viennese quack, but which I suspected were intended to foster a slight resemblance to Doc Brinkley, the goat gland man, who'd been a prominent citizen of Hot Springs before he hightailed it for Mexico. I hoped Hargis's medical credentials were less suspect than Brinkley's, but then this was just a narcotics cure and not heart surgery.

"By the way," the doctor said. "You'll need to get rid of all his medicine. Can't have any around the suite, not even hidden."

"You're not going to taper him off a little at a time?"

"No. This is what we call cold turkey. Cut him off all at once. It's not pleasant, but it's the most effective method we have. So take the pills and throw them away."

The doctor and his nurse went into Collins's room and I pocketed the rest of the old man's pills, close to three hundred probably. It sounded as though his bedside manner could stand some improvement; I first heard some muttering from Collins and then some garbled but loud introductions from the doctor, followed by a bellow of outrage from the old man. Anticipating a long evening, I told Park I was going out for some air.

At the Western Union desk I composed a telegram for Sally. I'd told her that Collins was coming down for a delicate medical procedure, that it was a secret, and that if anybody asked where I was she was to say Chicago.

"Is it one of those monkey gland deals?" she'd asked the morning we left. "Or is it goat glands?"

What the hell, it sounded plausible. "That's right, Doc Brinkley's coming back up from Mexico in secret to perform the operation. So you can see why he wants it kept quiet. Especially from Mrs. Collins. What would people think if they knew Everett Collins had the testicles of a goat?"

I saw Brinkley once on a gambling trip to Hot Springs before I got married. He hadn't been indicted yet, I don't think, and he strode down the sidewalk with the bearing of an archduke in miniature. His radio shows were a staple when I was a kid, promising rejuvenation and renewed virility through the miracle of interspecies ball exchanges. Not exchanges, really, since Doc Brinkley's operating theatre of horrors offered the poor goats nothing in return for the gift of their gonads. It might be argued that the human recipients of said testes received nothing either, since the most a transplanted pair of billygoat balls would get you was a nasty infection, and the doctor's death rates were high. The whole business reeked of charlatanism and the carnie sideshow and for years his program was by far the best thing on the radio.

I still listened to the Doc's radio shows at night sometimes, beamed northward from old Mexico at wattages forbidden to American broadcasters, and sometimes felt tempted to send in a dollar for an autographed photograph of Jesus Christ or a novelty box of jumping beans. Border radio never made me despair for civilization the way "Lum and Abner" or "Baby Snooks" did.

Once I'd sent the telegram I wandered down the street and found a saloon called the Inside Straight. I'd been expecting hillbilly music, but inside a five-piece Negro orchestra was doing a pretty good take on "Pussy Willow," and a decent looking gal greeted me as I walked in. At the bar I ordered a drink from a dapper bartender in a white tuxedo and took a look around the place. Expensive furniture and fixtures, and a mahogany backbar that looked like a survivor of the last century.

Standing there I fantasized that if I'd thought to bring my cash from the safety deposit box I might just take the company Olds and drive it down to Mexico myself for good, leaving everyone wondering whatever happened to good old Wayne instead of overseeing a drug fiend's unwilling detoxification and plotting to destroy another man's reputation or force him into retirement, a man who for all I knew was a decent, hardworking type who'd been careless about an exploitable peccadillo.

And then my bleak mood lifted of its own accord, as though I'd simply dwelt on it sufficiently to clear it out of my mind for a couple of days. I was in one of the most wide-open resorts in the country, surrounded by vice and shameless women. My expression must have changed because the bartender picked up on it and spoke.

"Here for the waters?" he asked in a Brooklyn accent thick as Durante's. He looked like a boxer, or maybe just someone people decided to punch in the face once in a while.

"Not particularly," I said.

"Hah. Didn't think so."

He didn't press me for more, a sign of a good bartender. All my visits to Hot Springs in the past had been on a markedly lower budget than this one, and now that Collins was in the care of a medical professional I began thinking about recreational possibilities.

"Where does a guy go to find a gal around here?"

"Depends if he's looking for a freebie or a paid piece of ass."

"In a strange place I always prefer to go for the latter."

"Smart man. Anything free around here is going to be very, very questionable. Where you staying?"

"The Arlington."

"Class operation, but don't ask for girls there, you'll pay too much." He wrote a number down on a matchbook. "Call this number and tell 'em Herb sent you."

"Thanks, Herb. How'd you end up down here, anyway?"

"Cousin of mine had some business associates down here. Speaking of which, you like to gamble?"

"Once in a while. I hate to lose." Having run a floating craps game in Italy I had come to realize that in gambling there wasn't much reason for the house to cheat, so stacked are the odds against any individual player.

"The place to go is the Hotel England, you ask for the management and tell 'em I sent you, they'll treat you all right."

"You're all right, Herb. Who's the gal up front?" I asked, nodding at the beauty greeting customers at the door.

"Vera's her name, I wouldn't waste time trying to get anywhere with her. Lots of guys have tried around here."

"Pretty girl."

"You're telling me. I'm a married man, but I'd give a year of my life for one night in the sack with her."

"It's just that I don't remember seeing any girls like her down here before the war."

"Not many like her now. She's from Little Rock, what passes for a city girl down here." He laughed. "Don't get me wrong, I'm not knocking the place, it's been good to me, and I can't go back to New York anyway. In fact, when I got down here I was knocked out by how swank it was. I was expecting Mammy and Pappy Yokum and donkeys in front yards and booze out of jugs marked XXX, if you know what I mean."

On my way out I said "Good night, Vera," and she responded with such familiarity and sweetness I almost stopped right then and there to ask her out for a drink later, but that was the wrong strategy for a girl like her.

AT THE HOTEL England the games were hopping, and a bigger orchestra than the one at the bar was tearing through "Main Stem." I asked for management and was pointed to a large, dark-haired man in a rumpled tuxedo who was gesticulating with his stogie to an apparently petrified subordinate, whom he then waved away with a delicate gesture of high-strung distaste.

"Herb sent me over," I told him.

"Herb, huh? How do you know Herb?" he asked.

"Just met him over at the Inside Straight."

"Oh, that's great, good old Herb." He said it with such relief it made me wish I knew why Herb couldn't go back to New York. "Here's the Herb special tonight." He handed me a two dollar chip. "Good luck, pal."

I decided right then that I was going to bet the two dollars and nothing I'd brought with me. At the roulette table I placed the chip on the red and won, then placed chips new and old on the black and won again. Then I took my winnings and dropped them into my jacket pocket, to the consternation of the dealer, who had plainly read me as a man who would let my bundle ride until it vanished with one wrong spin.

I played two hands of blackjack and won the second. Then I watched the craps table for a while to see if it was clean, since it was the only game I knew enough to judge by. It looked all right, but I'd watched so many craps tossed in the army the prospect of play held no joy for me. I was about to leave and spend my modest winnings on a steak dinner when I thought I saw someone I knew standing in front of a one-armed bandit. He didn't seem to have noticed me, so I cautiously moved around the silver row of machines and peered from the other end at my old army pal Lou Arnesdale.

He looked like shit stew warmed over the next day. His eyes were sunken and dull and he was thinner than he'd been in the army, so thin the army wouldn't have taken him back. He was playing one of the nickel machines and looking heartbroken every time the reels clanked once, twice, thrice to their sad resolution.

Lou Arnesdale owed me money, and from the looks of him he wouldn't be able to pay it back any time soon. We were partners in London selling army tires to civilians via a black marketeer named Syd, one of the sweetest deals I was ever in on, and I'd done Lou a favor letting him partner up with me. It turned out that Lou had a little narcotics habit of his own, and when he got transferred out of London he took over a thousand pounds of my money. That was pounds sterling, not dollars. He hadn't told me he was being trans-ferred and I wasn't able to track him down, and I certainly couldn't report the theft; some operations are off limits even by the standards of the Quartermaster Corps, and selling army rubber is definitely such an operation.

For a second I wondered if he was my poison pen correspondent, but it didn't seem likely. Lou'd known me in London, not Rome. Approaching him here was a non-starter, so I decided to take a position across the street and wait for him to come out. I didn't think it would take long, since the supply of nickels in his hand didn't amount to half a dollar, and his luck certainly wasn't going to get much better tonight.

I waved at the manager on my way out. "You win some and you lose some, huh?" I said.

"Better luck next time," he said, delighted to think that I'd dropped some of my own money at his tables.

THERE WAS A newsstand across the street. I browsed until I sensed the attendant getting antsy, then I bought the new *Esquire* and moved a few feet down the block. It was around eleven o'clock when Lou slinked out of the casino, dejected and friendless. He walked up that side of the street and turned a corner. I crossed and peered around it to make sure he wasn't looking back or waiting for me to catch up. He wasn't.

He continued up the street to a place called the Stuckey Palace Hotel and Apartments, a rundown brick building advertising weekly rates on the painted tin sign drilled into its facade. I waited until he'd had time to do whatever there was to do in the lobby, which would have differed depending on whether he was a hotel guest or a proper tenant. After five minutes had passed I stepped into a foyer and found no one on duty at the desk. Rows of mailboxes lined either side of the entry, beneath a panel affixed with the names and corresponding apartments of its inhabitants. ARNESDALE, L.P. lived in apartment 5H.

Retribution, whatever it turned out to be, could wait a few days. I'd waited years to find Lou and hadn't really expected ever to run across him. Now the gods had dumped him wriggling into my jaws, and I wouldn't waste the opportunity.

WHEN I GOT back to the hotel I called the number Herb had scrawled on the matchbook and had a girl sent up to my room. The service was cheap, as he'd promised, and mentioning his name had gotten me a further reduction in fee. When the girl showed up I let her into the room and she entered it with the élan and self-confidence of a movie star. She had jet-black hair pinned up at the crown of her skull and big black eyes that set off a slightly-too-large nose. Her walk had a nice sashay to it, and the first thing I asked after handing her the fee was for her to walk around the room a few times. When she asked me what I wanted next I told her to just get undressed and we'd think of something. She engaged me in some small talk as she performed her strip-tease, artfully tossing one garment after another over her shoulder or bending over to place it on a chair. I had a pretty good sense of her body before she'd finished and was glad I'd listened to Herb.

"What brings you to the Springs? Business or pleasure?" Her accent was northern Midwest, maybe the Dakotas, maybe Minnesota, maybe even Ontario, and I had to wonder what sad circumstance had brought her down to this hillbilly Sodom.

"Combination," I said. "Started with business, now there turns out to be some pleasure involved."

I was thinking of the pleasure I was going to get from killing Lou, but she took it for a compliment. "I'll try and keep you satisfied."

Fifteen minutes later a howling started coming from the supposedly soundproof suite next door. I didn't think the old man had been without his medicine for long enough to produce that kind of pain; possibly he was howling at the injustice of the whole business. He had become unaccustomed over the last thirty or thirty-five years to having his demands unmet or his orders disobeyed. Then again Dr. Hargis had mentioned that his particular methods involved the application of countermedications, and that the side effects of these were sometimes unpleasant.

"Do you hear that?" the girl asked, tensing beneath me.

"Yep," I said.

She pressed her hands to my chest to get me to stop pushing. "Shouldn't we do something? Call downstairs?"

"Trust me," I said, and I rode her another five minutes to the demented music of Everett Collins's wailing and yelling until I finally finished and rolled off of her.

"It sounds like someone's in pain," she said, sitting up.

"It isn't. The fellow next door is an animal trainer from the Clyde Beatty Circus. He's got Beatty's prize orang-outang, Rusty, in there."

"Aren't rangytangs dangerous?"

"Sure, but not this one. He's highly trained, brighter than most schoolchildren. But he's at the end of his life now, and they get senile just like people do. He probably thinks he's back in Borneo, running from a tiger."

"So Mr. Beatty put him up in a hotel?"

"He was very fond of this particular ape. Wanted him to end his days in luxury. Actually I believe he thought the waters might bring his reason back."

She narrowed her eyes, having caught me up. "You," she said. "You work for the circus, don't you?"

"I'm not really free to say one way or the other."

"Do you think there's any possibility Mr. Beatty is going to come and visit his monkey before he passes?"

"I couldn't say."

"My gosh, if he does, would you call back and ask for me? I love the circus. If I could have run away and done that I would have."

"I'll call you if he comes," I said, lacking the heart to disabuse her of whatever remained of the dreams of a Midwestern girl who'd run away and ended up joining a whorehouse instead of the circus.

THE NEXT NIGHT at eleven o'clock, having spent most of the day at the hotel playing cards with Herman Park and listening to Collins's screams, I stepped out onto the street. I'd only been out once, to the bus depot to meet a man the desk clerk had recommended as a source of illicit goods. The man was a strapping young hayseed who seemed not to have taken to farming. He wore his fedora at an angle meant to be rakish, but that made him look as though someone had recently knocked it askew without his noticing. His enormous Adam's apple danced as he spoke, and for the exorbitant price of fifty dollars he let me have a cheap revolver and a lead sap. Thinking that we were haggling, I'd made a counteroffer of thirty, expecting to pay forty, but he held firm. "Saps are illegal. You get caught selling a blackjack you could get time."

I was happy to get the sap as a backup plan. I figured on shooting Lou and making a run for it, but I worried about the noise, and I did like the idea of beating him to death with it, if I could get him unconscious quickly enough to avoid a lot of screaming. God knew I'd had enough of that for one day.

Now it was night, warm and humid, the sap weighing down my jacket pocket. The only time I'd ever used such a thing was in London, a token of esteem from Syd the black marketeer, who called it a cosh and described with unseemly gusto his favorite methods for its proper use.

Figuring it was probably still early for Lou to be returning I stopped in at the Inside Straight to thank Herb for his advice. Herb wasn't in, though, his replacement a taciturn rustic with ill-fitting dentures who served me my drink and scowled. The orchestra was the same but having an off night, plowing through Whiteman instead of swinging to Ellington, and the place had a dingy feel it hadn't had the night before.

The lovely Vera was still at the door, though, looking even better than the night before. I must have been pretty openly paying more attention to her than to the music, because the bartender finally spoke to me. "You'll never get anywhere with her. She's got no sex drive."

Did this toothless backwoods Adonis take any rejection from a female as evidence of lack of libido? I pressed him for details, expecting to hear a grudge-fueled hard-luck tale. Instead he gave me a real nugget of useful information.

"She's hooked on codeine. Spends a hell of a lot of dough on it, and it kills any desire she used to have to open her legs."

I finished my drink and headed for the door, and Vera tilted her head at me in disappointment as I left. I imagined I saw a bit of wooziness in her eyes, but that was probably the power of suggestion. "Just one tonight?" she asked, like a good hostess making sure to quickly learn the habits of anyone who showed the slightest sign of becoming a regular source of money spent.

"Just one," I said. "I'm Wayne, by the way."

"I'm Vera. But you know that."

"See you later," I said, and gave her a happy glance over my shoulder as I went.

BEFORE I HEADED out on the night's real business I headed up to my room to where I'd stashed Collins's remaining supply of Hycodan. Ten pills seemed about right for a start, and I headed back down to the street and hightailed it for Lou's.

A FEW MINUTES later I was standing outside the front of his building. I walked around the corner to examine the western facade; from the street there were no lights visible on the fifth floor. Once again there was no one to slip past at the front desk of the Stuckey Palace Hotel and Apartments, and I followed the path worn into the stairwell carpet up to the fifth floor. I'd brought a few things I thought might be useful for picking Lou's lock, but to my considerable surprise found that he hadn't locked his door. I looked around the apartment and found nothing of value; no doubt everything but his clothes had been pawned to feed his habit.

I turned out the lights again and sat down in Lou's threadbare easy chair and picked at the loose threads on the armrests. I hoped he wouldn't be too long; it wouldn't do for Lou to come home and find his would-be killer asleep in his front room.

Around twelve-fifteen the door cracked open and Lou entered. "Hello, Og. Long time," he said before he flicked the switch.

I had the revolver trained on his silhouette when the light came on. Lou was smiling.

"You robbed me, Lou. We were partners."

"No honor among thieves, Ogden, isn't that what they say?"

"Partners, Lou."

"What can I say? I had a monkey on my back the size of King Kong and dope peddlers after my hide and Uncle Sam offered me a transfer and I took it."

"Along with your money and mine."

"I know."

"And you still haven't kicked. All this time and you're still fixing, throwing all your money away."

"Nope, I kicked two years ago, after I got discharged. Dishonorable. You know how fucking hard it was to get a dishonorable discharge in the middle of that war? Damned hard."

"Doesn't look much like you kicked."

Another smile, rueful and without guile. There was forgiveness in it, fondness, even. "I did, though."

"Don't you want to know how I tracked you down?"

That smile again, patient and saintly. He looked seventy years old, and he was two years younger than I was. "Saw you last night at the casino, made damn sure you saw me."

"You wanted me to follow you."

"Yep. Came home an hour earlier than usual just so you'd know where to go."

Just then it hit me that he might be planning something of his own, but that look in his eyes belied any such notion. "You thought you could talk me into letting you off?"

He sank down into the recently vacated easy chair, seemingly exhausted. "Not at all."

"Then you know why I'm here."

"Og, I ain't hooked any more. I'm sick."

"Sick how?"

"Cancer. Plus I got the sugar diabetes so bad you could take my piss and make wine out of it. Course with the kidney troubles I don't produce much of that. One doc says I'm dead in three months, other one says I could last two years."

"So you think I'm going to give you a pass because you're sick."

"Hell, no. I'm expecting you to kill me, just like you meant to."

I stared at him and knew he was telling the truth. He winced from a sudden pain, clutched his side, a single shameful tear coursing down his stoic left cheek.

"I can't take two years of this, can't take three months even. Don't have the balls to do it myself. Jesus Christ sent you to me, Og. You're my angel of death."

"No, I'm not," I said, and I moved for the door. I nearly gave him the revolver and told him to be a man and do it himself, but in the end I just walked out the door without looking back, my revenge more severe than I'd pictured it and, curiously, less satisfying.

On my way through the lobby a poorly-shaven bald man called out to me. "All visitors must be announced," he said, his voice high in pitch and adenoidal. In a better mood I might have insulted his ancestry or told him where to go, maybe even broken his arm, but tonight I said nothing.

I WALKED AWAY in the wrong direction and ended up in a section of town even seedier than Lou's. Passing a dark doorway I was startled by the appearance of a raspy-voiced stranger.

"Help a fellow out?" he asked. I couldn't see him well but he was young and unshaven, and I almost reminded him that the depression was over. On second thought I pulled the gun from my coat and, after letting him get a good, long look at it, offered it to him, butt first. He stared without taking it.

"Go on, take it. Go earn yourself a living."

With some reluctance, even a smidgeon of fear, he took it and pocketed it. "Thanks, bub."

I turned and walked back in the other direction, toward the hotel. When I got to the Inside Straight I stopped back in and Vera greeted me by name, touching me ever so slightly on the sleeve as I passed her. I stopped as though an interesting but absurd thought had just come to me unbidden.

"Say, Vera, I don't suppose you ever get off work, do you? I'm here for a week with nothing to do." With an effort to appear casual I pulled a couple of Hycodans from my shirt pocket and displayed them before tossing them back out of sight.

She knew the pills by sight, and she gave me a look that on a less poised woman might have been described as brazen. "I do get off work, every night. Tonight included, if you're up late."

"I plan to be," I said, and I made up my mind to consider the rest of the week a vacation from all my cares.

VERA MADE THE week go by quickly and painlessly, for me at least, like one of those vacations where you start dreaming about setting up housekeeping. Her sexual appetite may have been diminished but her intense desire for more narcotics helped her pretend. The hycodan was more potent than the Mexican codeine she normally supplied herself

with, and within the week she'd lost some of that shimmering quality
in her eyes and even her hair seemed dulled and flattened, as if the dope
were leeching out the chemicals from her last permanent wave. When
I said goodbye I made her a gift of the remaining pills, a gesture that
prompted her to give me an address and a phone number in case I ever
passed through town again, but I didn't keep them. I didn't expect her
to be around if I ever got back.

THE DOCTOR HAD been paid and moved out the afternoon before we were
to leave, along with his nurse, and Collins was drinking gin and barking
insults and orders at me and Park both. There was no show of gratitude
for his involuntary cure, and though none was expected or required—we
were being paid for our trouble—the return of the old Collins wasn't
particularly agreeable. Once he'd availed himself of one of Hot Springs's
more expensive prostitutes—more expensive and less attractive than the
one I'd brought to my room that first night, just as Herb had warned—he
declared himself ready to return to Wichita and save his empire.

When the time came to go I elected to make the trip by train.
Park said nothing but I knew he resented having to drive all that distance weathering the old cocksucker's abuse. There seemed to be some
residual fogginess to Collins's demeanor from his months as a narcotics fiend—it didn't occur to him, for example, that he could make Park
drive and hire an airplane himself—but nothing sufficient to alarm the
board of directors, I didn't think, and most of the time it was camou-
flaged by his caustic disposition.

I WATCHED OUT the window as we passed through the bright green,
topographically complex southwestern Kansas terrain my father had

grown up in. It was coal mining country now, populated by Czechs
and Poles who'd moved there at the turn of the century to dig the
anthracite, but in his youth it had been nothing but farmland. Some
of my favorite boyhood memories were here, playing with cousins in
barns, lording it over them as a sophisticated boy from the big city,
on intimate terms with its gangsters and speakeasies. It was pure rot,
of course, but they all went to the picture shows and they pictured
Wichita as the very heart of urban sin and decadence. It struck me now
that if Wichita really was that way I'd be happy as a clam there; as it
was, the transition outside to the dull, flat plains of my own part of the
state inspired something akin to dread in my soul.

I got off at Union Station and had a porter haul my bags to a
taxi. The sun hadn't gone down yet when the cab pulled up in front
of my house, and I noted ruefully how badly the lawn needed mow-
ing. I resolved to canvas the neighborhood for some enterprising little
bastard who'd do it on the cheap and went around to the back and
unlocked the door, and upon entering was confronted by a musty odor
that suggested no one had been inside for a few days at least. I looked
around for a note and found none, and I supposed that Sally had gone
off to stay with my mother for a few days in my absence. I hadn't bothered wiring her to let her know I was coming home, so I really had no
beef about it. Still, it irritated me, coming home and having no dinner
on the table.

I drove out to Stanley's and ate a fried egg sandwich at the counter while listening to a snaggle-toothed lunatic next to me trying to
explain his theory about the earth shrinking after the detonation of the
A-bomb. In a decade the planet would be no bigger than the moon, in
a century no bigger than a beach ball. Then he laughed and explained

to me that it was no big deal, because the rest of the universe was contracting at exactly the same rate.

"So you see? None of it matters at all. It just seems like it."

I nodded and finished my egg sandwich, swigged down my coffee, and went home.

THIRTEEN
UP GO THE LEGS,
INTO THE AIR

I HAD A MESSAGE waiting for me when I got back to the plant. I was to call a Mr. Wageknecht about a German camera we'd been discussing. Mrs. Caspian gave me the message without meeting my eyes, as usual, and I took advantage of that to admire her ample form which, it seemed to me, was getting a bit more so.

"How are you these days, Mrs. Caspian? Is Mr. Caspian in town?"

Her face burned and she looked down at her typewriter, even though there was only one other person in the office, a skinny fellow with horn-rimmed glasses whose name I could never remember but who on hot days smelled like chicken soup.

"He's not," she said in a very small voice, appalled at my brazenness in speaking to her at the office. I felt like bending her over and taking her right there at the desk, right in front of no-name, but it could wait for that night. In that same small voice she continued, "I won't be working here any more after the fall."

"You won't?"

For the first time ever in the office she looked me straight in the face, her cheeks flushed and her eyes glistening. "Our prayers have been answered, Mr. Ogden. Mr. Caspian and I are expecting a baby."

"That's terrific," I said, though in fact I was disappointed to hear it, since it presumably meant that our liaisons would be coming to an end. "I've got to go take care of some business, maybe I'll see you before the end of the day."

I PHONED WAGEKNECHT from a phone booth at Central and Hillside. "I got all the pictures you want," he said. "Once your man Huff gets a drink in him he gets pretty sloppy."

"You know Red's? Out on 54?"

"Sure," he said.

"Be there tonight at eight. If the photos are what we want, you'll have your money."

I STOPPED BACK at the plant at four, mostly to see Millie Grau. Collins hadn't returned yet but was expected back late in the afternoon. Millie looked radiant, more so than usual, and I complimented her on it. "A lot's happened since you left. You were absolutely right about telling Donald about the baby. Oh, gosh, he was mad at me. He even called me a couple of names I wouldn't have thought he knew. But he prayed on it, and you know what? He decided to forgive me."

Forgive her? I had to work to keep my mouth shut right then. Some lousy sack of shit in a cassock has to talk to God to decide whether or not Millie Grau was worthy of him? Sight unseen, I already hated this clown's guts, but right then I wanted to bash his brains in with Millie's Smith Corona.

"That's great. Knew he'd feel that way."

"He says it's important for a modern couple to start life on an honest footing."

"Sure."

"You know, I think part of the reason he was mad was knowing we're not equally . . . experienced. He pictured me as a . . . " She stumbled over the word. "A virgin," she whispered.

"So he's never . . . " This time I stumbled, for want of a way to express such a thought acceptably to Miss Millie Grau.

"Never," Millie said. "And he's thirty. I know that's your next question."

It sounded like trouble to me. I considered telling her the story of John Ruskin being shocked into lifelong celibacy on his wedding night by the discovery that the genitalia of real women, unlike those in classical statuary, were hairy. But despite our recent conversational intimacy, I couldn't bring up pubic hair in her presence, even couched in the most prudish terms.

What the hell, I wouldn't feel right if I didn't say something. "Are you certain he's normal?"

"He's just very religious," she said without complete conviction. "And he never met the right girl before me."

He hasn't met the right one yet, I thought, and I halfway decided to do something about it before Millie made a big mistake, the kind you don't recognize until you're a few years down the road and fixing it isn't so easy.

PARK AND THE boss were back that afternoon at four. I told Park to go home and take a shower and get Collins to Red's by five. I wanted to see the look on his face when he saw the pictures. Park grumbled, but I told him it was Wageknecht with the candid shots and he shrugged. "Okay, that should be interesting at least."

We got a table at Red's and the old man was pointing at women and talking about which ones he wanted to screw and commenting on their looks and denigrating their male companions. It was like old times, one of those nights where I kind of liked the old reprobate.

"Look at that one, thinks she's sitting on a gold mine. In five years' time she's going to look like Eleanor Goddamn Roosevelt."

I saw Barbara the b-girl sitting at the bar with her arm in a sling. She saw me, too, but pointedly ignored me, presumably associating me with her lunatic assailant Rackey.

"So who's this coming to meet us?" Collins wanted to know.

"It's a surprise. Private dick I hired to get us some pictures."

Right then Wageknecht showed up at the door. He looked around for us, gave a little wave and headed in our direction. He was holding a manila envelope, and he slapped it on the table.

"I don't suppose you feel like looking at 'em right here," he said.

I took the envelope and peered inside. "That's the best part about Red's," I said, "Everybody minds his own damn business."

I pulled out one shot. It wasn't perfect, but you could tell it was Huff with someone in shadow, but definitely male, kneeling in front of him. "Close enough for government work," I said, and pulled another picture out.

"Show me, goddamnit," the old man said.

The next one was perfect: Huff on his knees, eyes closed in ecstasy and oblivious to the presence of Wageknecht's spy camera, the recipient of his attentions giving the lensman a coy, conspiratorial wink. I handed that one over to Collins and the first one to a very subdued, wide-eyed Herman Park.

Collins squinted, held the pictures at arm's length, then brought it very close to his face. "Is that . . ." Something like a smile was fighting its way to his lips, and he gave me a sidelong look. "This is a goddamn fake."

"Nope," Wageknecht said.

Collins let out a laugh that soared over the jukebox and drew the attention of half the bar. Park flipped the eight-by-ten over, even though no one was close enough to the table to see, and looked as though he desperately wished he were elsewhere.

"Ogden told me about this but I didn't believe it. What the hell. So Huff is a faggot after all." He looked over at Wageknecht.

"Looks that way," Wageknecht said, betraying no offense.

"Look at that son of a bitch. Goes to show you never can tell."

"They're all over the place," Wageknecht said. "Sometimes in disguise." He winked at Park, who looked away, shuddering.

Jerking his thumb at me he addressed Wageknecht. "How much is this cheap son of a bitch paying you, son?"

"Five hundred is what we agreed on."

Collins jerked a thumb at me. "Tomorrow he's going to give you another five hundred. And if we ever need a private dick again you're the one we'll call, not that fucking idiot Fish."

I handed him the envelope with the five hundred and told him I'd send the rest the next day.

"That's swell," he said. "Hope to work with you again some time." He was looking right at Park as he said it, and poor Herman looked like a gypsy'd given him the evil eye.

IT WAS NINE o'clock when we left, early enough for me to stop by Mrs. Caspian's apartment. When I rang the doorbell she answered wearing a baby blue peignoir, and was made up like a child's idea of a movie star, too heavy and too much color. Nonetheless, the fact that she was waiting for me gave me what I needed, and I pushed past her into her parlor. She grabbed my hand and led me into her bedroom and we screwed like I'd just gotten off of a desert island. She made even more noise than she had previously, and when we were finished we both lay there sweating and breathing hard.

"My God, Mr. Ogden, what are we going to do about the baby?" she said, the first words she'd spoken since I walked in the door. "My husband hasn't touched me in months."

"Does he know about it yet?"

"No, not yet. He's coming home this weekend."

"Okay, here's what you do. Get all dolled up like you did for me tonight, and when he gets home you get him in bed under any pretext possible. Rape him if you have to, you're a good strong gal. How far along are you?"

"It's two months, I think."

"Perfect. A month from now you tell him he got you pregnant, and seven months from now when the baby comes tell him you're in premature labor."

"But the doctor won't like that. He won't lie for me."

"I'll find you one who will," I said. Odds were Dr. Groff knew a bribable obstetrician. Hell, those guys probably had to lie for their patients all the time. "We'll get through this, Mrs. Caspian, and once the baby's here we'll keep meeting like before. Trust me on this."

She sniffed. "I do. You're a wonderful man, Mr. Ogden."

THE NEXT DAY I slept late, and when I got up I typed out a letter to Mr. Huff on Sally's portable Remington.

Mr. Huff,

Some of us think things are going along just fine at Collins. Others seem to think Mr. Collins's time is through. We would be most grateful for your support at this time, and any influence you might exert over those members of the board inclined to displace him.

Yours,

(signed)

Wayne Ogden

Maybe the letter should have been anonymous. After all, as far as I knew, I was committing a felony. But the risk inherent in using my name and Collins's was outweighed by the value of reminding Huff that we had the upper hand in the matter. From now on he was playing for our side.

I noted at the bottom that there was an enclosure and placed the glossy eight-by-ten along with the letter in the same manila envelope Wageknecht had provided.

I RECOGNIZED HUFF's secretary from that brief period before the war when I used to actually perform a useful function in the publicity and marketing department. A dour middle-aged woman with thin hair arranged in a fluffy, transparent nimbus that from certain angles allowed glimpses of bare scalp, I remembered that though she was a sourpuss she could be gotten to with a joke. I told her the one about the priest and the rabbi and the minister and St. Peter, just about the only clean one I knew, and she laughed. Then I asked to see her boss.

"What about? He's pretty busy today."

"I have something to give him personally. Charged to do so by the Big Man himself."

"I can give it to him."

"Mr. Collins insists. I don't mind waiting."

She probably didn't want to hear any more stupid jokes, because she got up and went into Huff's office. A minute later he came out, looking distracted and impatient.

"Here you go," I said. "Mr. Collins wanted you to have this."

He took it without a word and went back into his office.

That night I finally phoned Sally at my mother's house to let her know I was back. She was frantic, and I couldn't tell if she was mad at me or scared or both.

"A pervert called me and asked for you, and when I told him you were out of town on business he said he was going to come over and do something terrible. Didn't you get my telegram?"

"No. What did he sound like?"

"Like one of those telephone perverts. And he said he'd been watching me, he told me what I was wearing that morning and he got it right. I think he got a big kick out of thinking he scared me, so I just pretended to laugh and told him I'd cut off his tiny shriveled little thing if he showed."

That was Sally, all right. If the army had taken women for combat units she would have been a natural. "I mean did he sound young? Old? Like a southerner or someone from around here?"

"He sounded like one of the Bowery Boys in the movies."

"Don't worry about it, baby. Those perverts are usually harmless," I told her, and I was thinking that when I finally met up with my pen pal I might just follow Sally's plans and carve a little piece of the son of a bitch loose.

THE PHONE RANG in the morning and I didn't answer it. I was shaved and dressed and didn't want to wait for Sally to make breakfast so I knocked on the bathroom door and told her I had a meeting to go to. There was no sign on the street of anybody watching the house: no suspicious cars, no strangers hiding in the trees, no men in trenchcoats and dark glasses, so I got into the car and backed out of the drive.

Fifteen minutes later I was at Stanley's reading the morning *Beacon*'s account of a three-car wreck on West 54 that left eight dead, listening to a jovial, well-dressed fat man three stools down besmirch the honor of the counterman's sister.

"There must be something wrong with the way your folks raised her," he said, voice loud and urgent.

"Same as me and the others," the counterman said. He was lean and wiry with big bony fists, and I was thinking the fat man might want to temper his comments. "We all came out all right." He didn't seem too bothered by the attack on his sister's reputation.

The place was empty at that hour—it was ten o'clock by the time I got out of the house—which was a good thing, because the fat man was getting pretty wound up, and a large audience might have inhibited him. "It's like she can't help herself. She sees a man she takes a shine to, up go the legs, into the goddamn air."

"Just her nature, Sylvester," the counterman said with a philosophical shrug.

"I never seen any woman wasn't getting paid for it lay down for that many men. Milkman. Mailman. The goddamn paper boy! I don't think the little bastard even shaves yet. And it's not like she gets any free milk or a few weeks of free newspapers out of it. A woman her age."

Now there was a gal I wanted to meet. When he looked down, dejected, at his untouched plate of eggs I realized that he hadn't been needling the counterman at all; he was seeking sympathetic ears, the woman under discussion his own errant wife. It didn't seem to me like things were going to improve short of locking the woman in question in a mental institution.

"She wasn't ever like this before the war," he said, piercing the thin albumen skin of one of the yolks with his fork and then pressing it flat to watch the molten yellow ooze out of the jagged rifts. "Used to be a pretty good wife."

I walked into Collins's office before noon and found Millie sitting behind her desk, eyes red. Assuming that her problem had to do with her fiancé, I took a seat across from her desk and asked what was wrong. If I was going to pound him into the dirt I wanted to know why, exactly.

"Oh, Mr. Ogden, you haven't heard? It's just awful. Last night Mr. Huff got into his garage and closed the door and started his car and went to sleep."

Shit. This was a bad change in plans. "I need to talk to his secretary," I said.

"She's not there, she had to go home. She's very upset. And the county attorney's got the office sealed, there are policemen there keeping people out."

"Sure, I guess they have to take precautions when the comptroller kills himself."

"Oh, nobody thinks he did anything improper. It's a routine thing, they said."

Shit. If that letter and the photograph were still in the same envelope I was doomed. Huff had screwed us but good; it hadn't occurred to me that the son of a bitch might overreact and finish himself off. I'd counted on having him as an ally in the fight with the board, if a reluctant one, and now there was the danger Collins and I might be tied to a blackmail attempt.

"How's his wife doing?"

"I don't know. She's taken the boys somewhere, to a relative I think. It's just awful."

"Where's the boss?"

"He went home as soon as he found out. He was very upset. He pretended not to like Mr. Huff, but I know he's taking it very hard."

PARK MET ME at Red's at five. "You really stepped into the shit this time, Ogden." He said it like he was mad at me personally.

"We need to find out where that photo ended up. If he burned it we're in the clear. If it's separate from the letter we're as good as clear, it'd take a hell of a lawyer to put that case together. But if they're still in the same envelope . . . "

"I'm not doing it." He was sitting with his arms folded across his chest.

"I haven't asked you to do anything yet. We're here to figure out how we're going to find out what he did with the picture."

"Not me. I'm here to quit."

"Quit? Over what?"

"That man Huff killed himself because of that stunt we pulled. It's not right. I'm not a cop any more but I can't let myself be involved with felonies."

"What the hell, Park, you're going soft on me all of a sudden?"

He shook his head at me. "I can hardly stand the sight of you."

I'm wrong once in a while about all kinds of things, but one thing I almost always get right is who my friends are, and in this case it sure threw me to have been wrong. I reached into my pocket and pulled out my wallet, counted out two hundred dollars in fifties and handed them to him.

"That's your severance pay, Herman," I said. "Good luck in the future."

He rose, slugged back his shot and washed it down with half his beer. Then he threw the bills onto the bar and walked away.

THE EVENING EAGLE played the story down, describing the death as accidental in a single column on page four. The Beacon's late edition played it big on the front page above the fold, quoting the county attorney as saying it looked like a suicide and even suggesting the existence of a note. There was even the merest suggestion of a double life Mr. Huff might have been leading, though what sort of double life was left to the imagination of the reader.

Millie had spoken of Huff's wife taking their sons to stay with relatives. Huff's office was sealed while the county attorney and the CPAs looked over the books, but would his house be sealed as well? It was worth a try. The *Eagle*'s brief article had published his College Hill address, and at nine I drove past a large, darkened, two-story house and saw no evidence anyone was home. Of course Mrs. Huff might have been the sort to retire early, particularly the day after her husband's death, but I felt reasonably sure the house was empty. If it wasn't I'd find out soon enough.

At midnight I returned and parked two blocks away on Roosevelt. I walked down the sidewalk with as much nonchalance as a midnight stroller has any business feeling, and when I arrived at the house I walked around back as quietly as I could. At the end of the driveway stood the garage where Huff had done it; if the envelope was in the car at the time of the suicide then it was likely the police already had it, and if by some miracle it was still in there untouched I would have to raise the garage door to get to it, difficult if not impossible without making an attention-getting racket. So I would leave that until after my search of the house, as a last, desperate resort.

I wrapped my handkerchief around my fist and broke a glass pane in the door, stuck my arm through, and unlocked it. I crept through the kitchen and turned on my flashlight, careful to aim it low lest its beam alert an insomniac neighbor. A grey cat with extremely thick fur and a flat face meowed at me and purred, rubbing itself against my ankles, and I opened the refrigerator and put some milk in its empty bowl.

I climbed the stairs and examined the bedrooms. There were three, one occupied by the adults and two others filled with the accoutrements of children, specifically boys. In the hallway were family pictures indicating that there were four of them, and in the most recent of these the boys ranged from about a gap-toothed, towheaded six to a surly, crew cut fifteen.

I returned downstairs. At the rear of the house next to the kitchen was a small room Huff had apparently been using as an office. I went through the desk and found nothing of use, and was about to leave when I saw something on the wall: It was my letter, stuck there by thumbtack, as though he had sat there contemplating it before his act of self-destruction. Unaccompanied by that letter, the photo was powerless to do me or Collins harm, and it was with an audible sigh that I tore it from the wall and stuffed it in my shirt. And then I spotted something that might have been the corner of a piece of typing paper overhanging the corner of a bookcase. I reached for it; it was stiffer than typing paper, and sure enough, flipping it over I found Huff's picture. The inconsiderate son of a bitch had left it lying around where his wife, or one of his sons, was eventually bound to find it. I did him a favor and took it and, as I let myself out, wondered whether Merle Tessler in Kansas City would be interested in getting Wageknecht's negatives. There was a market for everything, why not this?

FOURTEEN

ON PROPOSITIONING
A WIDOW

"THERE WAS A gal I met barnstorming, had a trick snatch."

We were at Norman's, and Collins was at the garrulous stage of his nightly inebriation. "Trick how?" Norman said, his tone full of awe. He had known nothing but standard issue pussies in his sheltered life, and even those seemed to him miraculous.

"She worked for the carnival. I'd run into her two, three times a year, and she was always up for it. Liked pilots. Liked pretty much anything in pants, probably."

"I thought you said women who needed more'n one man were nuts," Norman said. "Ants in the pants equals rocks in the head."

"She was an exception," the old man said, showing a bit of the prickliness that was sure to surface fully blown by evening's end; I really did need to find a successor to Herman Park before long. "Her name was Carlotta, or at least that was what she was calling herself then. Probably used to be Ethel or Laverne or Myrtle until she joined the carnie. Anyhow, she could squirt cold cream out of it and hit you right in the goddamn face. Shit, if they could have sold tickets to it they could have made some real kale. And boy oh boy, fucking her was like fucking no other woman alive. She pretty much ruined me. I suppose I've spent the rest of my life searching for another woman like that."

"So how'd you end up married to Mrs. Collins?" Norman asked without apparent fear of getting an earful of abuse in return. I couldn't quite figure out whether Norman simply hadn't learned how to avoid tetchy subjects with Collins, or whether he just didn't mind the abuse the old geezer piled on him.

But for once Collins's reply was gentle, rueful even. He sketched a vision of young Mrs. Collins as a beautiful Irish colleen, only a generation removed from County Mayo. Splendid to look at, with a quiet disposition he took to be shyness. At that point he was tired of barnstorming, setting the stage for the first incarnation of Collins Aircraft Company in a converted barn in Saginaw, and he thought it was time to marry. It wasn't until after the wedding that he realized that what had seemed timidity was in fact just a generalized dislike of humanity. "I would have caught on to her before I married her except she drove me temporarily crazy."

"Crazy how?" Norman asked.

"She wouldn't let me touch her. 'That's for marriage, Everett.' And when I say no touching I'm not talking about having her suck my cock or even getting a quick feel of her tits, either. I'm saying she wouldn't let me touch her on the shoulder or the arm. And she had a hell of a figure, too, in those days. These days she looks like a two-hundred-fifty-pound Sister of the Blessed Virgin Mary with a droopy left eye and a cane, but back then I'd have given a year of my life for a night with her. And you know, for once in my life I thought I loved someone. So on our wedding night I found out that she thought sex was a damned chore and strictly necessary for the production of babies, and once I'd popped a load in her she said that's it until next month."

Driving back to the east side of town Collins was so agitated I was beginning to think some of the effects of those months on Hycodan might be permanent. He blamed me for Park's defection, and all the way out there he grumbled about how I was a shit excuse for a driver and no bodyguard at all.

"And Huff isn't supposed to be dead, he's supposed to be working for us now," he said.

I reminded him that he'd signed off on the plan, that he'd been delighted to see the incriminating photograph.

"Doesn't matter. Now I've got to go to the goddamn funeral and act like I'm sorry the son of a bitch is dead. And I still don't know how the board's going to vote. He didn't have a vote, you know."

"I know."

"Shit, who knows if he could have changed any of theirs."

"There are still ways of influencing votes."

"How? You going to dig up the goods on the whole board? In a week's time?"

"I'm working on it."

SINCE HE LEFT no note there was no proof Huff had put out his own lights, so he got a funeral mass at St. Bridget's of Galway. The large crowd was a testament to the popularity Minnie Grau had spoken of, and I was surprised to see that the officiating priest was none other than my old childhood pal Joe McGill. I hadn't seen him since before the war and though he'd grown a little rounder and slightly bald, there was still a childish air about him, as though he were merely posing as a priest and terrified someone was going to catch him out in his masquerade.

Huff's sons sat with their mother, the youngest one crying silently and the older ones ranging in aspect from sullen anger to shell shock. They looked like fine boys, and I was proud to have spared them the discovery of the eight-by-ten. The newly minted widow was surprisingly attractive, younger looking in person than in the family photographs hanging in her upstairs hallway; perhaps a rejuvenating effect of the dark veil. She had nice legs, tapering down to a pair of heels that, even in black, were perhaps a little high for a funeral. Dr. Freud would have said she was sending out a subconscious signal, seeking some of the sexual attention she had certainly been missing for the last few years, and I wondered what Emily Post had to say about how soon after a funeral it was proper to proposition a widow.

In the audience I spotted several board members, including Lamarr, Burress, and Latham. A well-lobbed grenade would have taken care of our problems right then and there, and I felt a pang of nostalgia for my quartermaster days. If they'd been a trio of inconvenient bird colonels back in the European Theater of Operations it would have happened, though not without some complications for your trusty supply sarge. Ordinance, of course, was the trickiest item in a black marketeer's inventory, since it was more strictly accounted for than morphine or liquor, and since the QM Corps didn't handle it ourselves a dangerous bargain would have to be made, but for those three turdapples I would have pulled it off.

Lamarr squirmed in his pew like a man infested with a crippling dose of the crabs, his eyes bulging and wild, forehead glistening with sweat, the inch-thick layer of suet beneath his skin turning it the color of clotted cream. His demure, pretty wife sat next to him with her gloved hands in her lap and ignored him, never guessing how lucky she was to be married to a banker and not an army officer.

Collins sat toward the front, looking solemn next to Mrs. Collins, who looked the way I imagined she always must have in church: deep in contemplation of the divine mysteries of creation, first and foremost among these being why a just God would unite indivisibly one of his most pious and chaste creations with a syphilitic, drunken, promiscuous heathen of a husband.

Toward the back sat Millie Grau, wiping her eye with the corner of a handkerchief. To her left was a stiff with a clerical collar and slick blond hair, arms folded across his chest and avoiding her touch so scrupulously that I knew it was Donald. He looked as though the sound of the Latin mass and its attendant papist pageantry was tormenting his Lutheran soul to the point of distraction, and at several points in the proceedings I saw him blow out exasperated sighs.

The sound of Joe's Latin didn't suit me, either, though for different reasons. Having been raised by a classics scholar and freethinker I had rarely ever had occasion to hear church in Latin, and my old pal's pronunciations sounded outright wrong to my ears. This was unfortunate, because it inspired an inappropriate urge to laugh, and I forced myself to conjugate verbs in Greek in order to drive the other language from the forefront of my mind. I hoped the concentration on my face read to my fellow mourners as pained supplication for the safe passage of Huff's soul heavenward.

J.T. Burress stood up in the middle of the proceedings and headed for the rear. I followed him, having paid all the respects I considered due. Outside Burress stood smoking a cigarette and looking agitated. He must have flown in from New York, and I didn't imagine he was happy about the prospect of two airplane trips to Wichita inside of a month. His suit was too heavy for a Kansas day in May, and he looked like he was about to drop. He had on the only pair of pince-nez glasses I'd seen in years, and he glanced over at me as though trying to place me. Most likely he'd seen my picture in whatever reports he'd been getting from Huff or Lamarr or Latham, whichever of them had been doing the grunt work in the effort to oust the boss and me.

"Heck of a thing, isn't it?" I said as I approached.

"Certainly is. Man in his prime like that." He hawked up a little bit of phlegm and, after a moment's silent debate, swallowed rather than spit on the church steps in front of the hearse driver and some stranger.

"Wonder what made him do it?"

"It was an accident. If it weren't we wouldn't be standing outside a Catholic church, I'll tell you that." He looked away, turning slightly so that there could be no mistaking his intentions. The conversation was over. Maybe he'd figured out who I was, or maybe he just didn't like my looks, or maybe it was the shit-eating dopey grin I'd put on for his benefit.

Old J.T. had been a friend of Collins's since the founding of the company, one of the first financiers to put money into the enterprise, and I almost admired the sangfroid with which he'd turned on his old pal. He looked like he hadn't taken a good dump in years, like he was just counting the days until he was laid out like Huff, like the only joys he had left were screwing over friends and attending funerals.

DINNER THAT NIGHT was another abomination from a ladies' magazine, involving a can of cream of mushroom soup, some undercooked potatoes, and a very bad cut of beef boiled into tastelessness, the whole thing seasoned with a great deal of salt. I suspected my dear wife of improvisation, since no sane editor could have allowed such a recipe into print as she had prepared it. I ate about a third of it like a soldier, avoiding the hardest of the potato chunks and complimenting her resourcefulness. When I was done she looked defeated and small, and I assured her it had been delicious. "I've got to take the old man out to a roadhouse later," I said.

"How come he can't drive himself?"

"Because he gets drunk when he goes out, and if he got killed I'd be out of a swell job."

"How come somebody else can't drive him?" she wanted to know.

It was a good question, especially since I wasn't really driving the old man around that night, having managed to pawn the job temporarily off on the equally heavy-drinking Rackey. Probably Collins would have been better off driving his own car, but I wasn't worried about that tonight.

"It's just until we hire a new bodyguard. And I'll be home as early as I can."

She pouted, and I couldn't get a kiss out of her as I left. That was all right; if she was mad she wouldn't wait up.

I DROVE DOWNTOWN and met Irma and Wageknecht at the Bellflower Café and ordered some chop suey to make up for Sally's inedible meal. The chop suey was lousy as ever, but by comparison it went down pretty well.

"It's real white of you to call me in on this," Wageknecht said.

"The old man promised you you'd get first crack at anything like this, and he keeps his word."

"I been thinking maybe I could get me a license and do this kind of work full time," he said. He looked at Irma. "Maybe you could be my gal Friday."

"Nice try, I'd rather earn my money on my back than sitting in front of a typewriter all day." She ground her cigarette into the ashtray and gave a little snort.

"Then you could be my partner. Like Myrna Loy and William Powell."

"Sure, only difference is Powell's not fucking her, he's chasing Cary Grant instead."

I was quiet, wolfing down the chop suey. I signaled the girl to bring me another plate of it while they mapped out their new careers. Finally I stopped eating for a minute and added my two cents.

"I don't know shit about the detective business, but you could sure make some money taking dirty pictures. Nester could find some way to distribute them through the mail."

They looked at one another and nodded slowly at the wisdom of my suggestion, scenarios brewing independently in their heads and growing into the seeds of a new enterprise, the future source of a million lonesome orgasms all across this land. I felt like I'd done them a favor, getting them off of this detective nonsense, which was a sure-fire waste of time and energy.

"All right then. You brought the 35 millimeter job?" I asked Wageknecht.

"Brought the Speed Graphic with a flashgun. I figure if you mostly want to intimidate this guy, the Speed Graphic is a scarier camera."

"Good thinking. The picture will be better, too, if we actually have to use it, which I very much doubt. Are we all ready, then? Everybody know their part?"

IT WAS NEARLY ten thirty when we walked two blocks down to the Eaton, where Burress had a top floor suite. That made it eleven thirty Eastern time, and I assumed that Burress kept conservative hours. Jerry the hotel dick was waiting for us by the kitchen entrance, and when I handed him his envelope full of cash he grinned. "You're trouble, Ogden, but I like your style. Always a little something extra."

We went up the service elevator and Wageknecht and I waited outside in the corridor while Jerry quietly opened the door to the suite and let Irma in. Then he went back down the service elevator, pausing to give a jaunty little salute as the doors closed. Strictly speaking I shouldn't have been on the scene, but I had to see the look on the smug son of a bitch's face when he realized the game was up.

Two minutes later Irma gave the signal, an eardrum-crippling whistle of the two-fingers-in-the-mouth variety, a skill I'd never mastered myself. We hurried in to find a bewildered J. T. Burress on the floor of the bedroom in his nightshirt, straddled by Irma, who wore only bra, panties, and black stockings.

"Say 'cheese,'" Wagknecht said, just to be an asshole, and he took the picture, the bulb in the flash gun exploding a little louder than seemed right. Burress was looking at me, and there was a dim sort of recognition in his eyes.

"You were . . . " he said, pointing his finger at my face, "I saw you today . . . " With that his eyes went wild and he yelped in pain.

"Oh, shit," Irma said. "I've been around for this before."

She picked up the phone and dialed. "Jerry, you'd better call an ambulance, there's a guy up here having a heart attack."

I drove them over to Norman's. He was drinking alone and glad to have some company. Irma and Wageknecht were both in a funk, and once he'd heard the story Norman tried to cheer them up.

"You did good, it sounds like to me," he said.

"That's the way I see it," I said. "If he lives, we've got a hell of a picture to send him. If he doesn't, the problem's solved a different way."

Wageknecht wasn't sold on it. "I don't think I'm cut out for the detective business, if everyone I tail ends up dying."

"It's just two of them, and we don't even know about Burress yet."

Irma was quiet, and kept handing her glass back to Norman for more. "I kinda like the old guys. They're generous."

"Not this one, I'll bet. He's a goddamn banker, probably keeps his own dough stuffed inside his mattress."

Norman perked up at the news that Irma liked old guys. "You know, one thing about us old guys is, we take our time and don't jizz quite so quick as all that." Irma and Wageknecht looked at one another, eyebrows raised.

During the solitary portion of his evening Norman had gotten a pretty serious head start on his drinking, and he wasn't doing a very good job concealing his devotion to his new friend Irma. He was wobbling a little bit even in his sitting position, and when he got up to open a new bottle he had to lean against the wall on his way across the room. Upon his return he refreshed Irma's glass first, and then knelt in front of her as if to propose marriage, which wouldn't have surprised me at that point.

"Do you know that you bear a very strong resemblance to the motion picture performer and artiste . . . " Here he had to stop and collect his thoughts momentarily. " . . . Miss Joan Blondell, whom I consider to be the most sweet and attractive of all the stars in . . . " Another pause came, and he closed his eyes and furrowed his brow. " . . . all Hollywood's firmament?" This last word came at a cost of some effort, but he added no extra syllables and seemed quite pleased with himself once he'd finished.

Irma looked pleased, too, flushed and newly radiant, and she leaned down and touched her hand to his cheek. I don't think he could have been more thrilled if it had been a handjob. "Maybe we could arrange a date sometime," she said, and she rummaged through her handbag for a calling card.

"I would like that very much, Miss," Norman said, accepting the card as though it were a gift of great price. I was pretty sure we had established earlier in the evening the nature of Irma's profession; her resemblance to Joan Blondell had cured him of his aversion to paying for it, which would probably result in his being a happier man. Now he turned to Wageknecht. "And what is it you do for a living, young fellow?"

"I'm a private detective," he said, trying the phrase on like a costume. "I used to be a whore, though."

Norman nodded, looking like the idea was new to him. "That's interesting."

Wageknecht nodded. "And if the private detective business doesn't work out, I'm thinking about taking dirty pictures and selling them."

Norman smiled. "That's a job I would have loved to have when I was younger," he said.

"How serious are you about giving it up?" I asked Wageknecht.

"Pretty serious."

I thought for a minute before I spoke again. It seemed perfect. Collins might object to Wageknecht if he knew about the whole queer business, but there was no reason for him to find out unless Wageknecht told him. And he was an ex-marine. "Wageknecht, how would you like a job as a bodyguard and chauffeur?"

"Hell, yes, I'd like it."

"All right then, show up at Collins Aircraft tomorrow at eleven and I'll take you down to personnel."

"That's swell of you, Mr. Ogden."

"I believe I'd rather have that job taking dirty pictures," Norman said, and not long after that he fell asleep.

DRIVING HOME AT three-fifteen in the morning I felt as though I hadn't slept in a week, and I was ready to surrender to Morpheus. I cursed, then, when I spotted an unfamiliar vehicle parked two houses south of mine, a '34 or '35 Chrysler Airflow with New York MD plates, an absurdly conspicuous choice for a driver who wanted to keep his profile low.

Of all the nights for this shit-for-brains to show up in person, he'd picked tonight. The adrenaline that had pumped through my system earlier in the evening came back in force, and my fatigue evaporated. I turned at the next intersection and doubled back, parking one street west on South Volutsia. I cut between two houses and watched the Airflow for five or six minutes and satisfied myself that the driver, his head back and his mouth open, was asleep. Then I went back to the Olds and drove around the block again.

This time I backed into the driveway and slammed the door when I got out. I didn't dare sneak a look backward at the Airflow, but I hoped my arrival had startled him awake. Feigning a drunken stagger as I made my way up to the front door, I made a show of fumbling with my keys and stumbled inside, leaving the door open.

Sally was a good, solid sleeper, but I hoped I wouldn't have to explain to her what was happening. In a crouch, I made my way to the fireplace and grabbed an andiron, one with a nice sharp hook at the end of it, and took a position over by the front door.

A silhouette appeared, holding a gun in one hand and a satchel in the other. He moved gingerly into the room, illuminated by the lone streetlamp outside, and as soon as he crossed the threshold I brought the andiron down hard on the back of his head, and when he hit the ground I hit him again in the face.

I got some copper wiring and a large oilskin tarp from the garage and tied his wrists and ankles with the wire before wrapping him in the tarp, then locked him in the trunk of the Olds. I took his gun, a .38, and his satchel, which was made of leather and marked with the initials WGP MD, and put them in the car, then cleaned off of the linoleum and threw the bloodied dishrag into the big trash can in the garage, piling some newspapers over it in case Sally might take a load of kitchen waste out. Then I took my trusty old wheelbarrow and a shovel and, as quietly as I could, loaded them into the backseat of the Olds.

I got behind the wheel and headed out to highway 54. Just outside the little town of Augusta was an old limestone quarry where my dad used to take me looking for fossils when I was a boy. I was hoping that the abandoned foreman's shack was still standing; even if it wasn't, there wasn't a house within two miles of the place. At least there didn't used to be.

Fifteen minutes later I was pulling into the quarry road. I hoped my bashful correspondent wasn't dead, because I wanted to find out a few things before he checked out.

I shone my flashlight into his leather satchel: inside was a sadist's bounty of torture tools: knives, pliers, duct tape, and an assortment of medical supplies, including syringes and surgical instruments and small bottles of drugs. It seemed impossible that my tormentor was a doctor, given the analphabetical quality of his notes, but that may have been a ruse.

I took the wheelbarrow and shovel from the back seat, opened the trunk, and heaved the oilskin bundle into the barrow. It let loose a grunt when it hit, and I loaded the medical bag and copper wire on top of it. Then I marched to the foreman's shack, halfway around the rim of the quarry with the shovel balanced over my shoulder and the .38 in my pocket, the wheelbarrow bouncing and jiggling in the dark, the flashlight's beam shining crazily over the path ahead.

I dumped the barrow out when I got to the foreman's shack and hauled him inside. Very carefully I untied the wire that held the ends of the tarp closed and found that he was breathing.

From his back trouser pocket I took his wallet and learned that he was not a doctor, nor were his initials WGP. His driver's license identified him as Ralph Joseph Gardner, of Astoria, Queens, New York, as did a Veteran's Administration Employee's Identification card. Apart from a Social Security card and seven dollars, that was all the wallet contained.

With the flashlight in his squirrely eyes I knew him right away. He was a PFC who'd tried to sell me a stolen army jeep in Rome, gap-toothed in front and sunken-chested, who walked with a peculiar stiff-legged gait as though he was imitating John Wayne. "Hell, you're a fence, ain'tcha?" he'd said, insulted that I wouldn't fork over for a set of wheels that would have got me court martialed. I remembered him spending lots of his pay on whores, though not whether he was particularly attached to one girl or another.

I considered the possibility of killing him right then and disposing of him somehow before the sun came up. I was still curious about him, though, about how he'd settled on me as the villain in his imaginary love story, so I slapped him in the face, hard. He stirred, his eyes unfocused and bleary, and then he got a load of me and tried to yell. Only a hoarse rattle came out, though, and I thought maybe I'd knocked him stupid.

"How are you, Ralph?"

"Go to hell." He was slurring, but I didn't think he was drunk.

"So what's your beef with me? Still mad about that jeep?"

"Lemme go," he said, pulling at the wire.

"I didn't kill Brunela, you know. She killed herself."

"Same as. Lousy pimp. She loved me."

"She was a pro. She didn't love you."

"She listened to me. She was going to come to America with me when the war was over."

"Brunela fucked you for money, just like she did a thousand other guys. She listened to your sob stories because you were paying her to. And I didn't kill her."

"You pimped her."

I shook my head, exasperated at his refusal to face reality. "But I didn't turn her out. She'd been working two or three years already by the time I came on the scene. The fact is I improved her working conditions. Made her last six months or so bearable, the way I see it."

The funny thing about it was, old Ralph didn't seem very scared. He was pissed off, sure, but I really don't think he'd figured out that his number was up. "You think the rules don't apply to you, Ogden. Just the rest of us."

"I can't quite figure you out," I said. "You're smart enough to track me down halfway across the country, and dumb enough to fall in love with a hooker."

"And you cheating Uncle Sam while guys like me was getting killed fighting."

"Ralph, you were stealing jeeps from the army. And I see you're still stealing cars. I'm guessing the Airflow and the bag both belong to one of your Administration docs. How'd you find me, anyway? I know you work for the VA, but I can't believe they'd let an illiterate work as a file clerk."

"I got a lady friend in the filing department, helps me out."

"Shit, Ralph, you should have been satisfied with that. A job and a girl, that's the American dream. You probably would have had your own car before long. House with a lawn. Now what have you got to look forward to?"

"Going to make you pay for what you did to Brunela. And then I'm going to fuck that wife of yours. She's some potato."

"You mean tomato, you dumb shit." I was tired of the sound of him and tired of the sight. He was just about to say something when I picked up the shovel.

"Hey, wait. You can't kill me."

"Sure I can," I said, and I dragged him by the legs out the broken doorframe of the shack. He was struggling pretty hard and I thought I'd better shut him down quickly, so I swung the shovel over my shoulder like a golfer. That finally put a scare into him, and he let loose a terrified wail as I brought the blade down sideways and hard on his head. His piteous wail didn't end with the impact but wound down over two or three seconds, like a radio that's been turned off.

A dozen yards from the shack I began to dig.

FIFTEEN
SAUL OF TARSUS

JUST BEFORE DAWN I drove the Airflow and left it in front of Ketteman's bakery with the doctor's bag locked in the trunk. I didn't owe him, but I felt a certain kinship since we'd both had a beef with Ralph. They'd get back to him eventually. The adrenalin hadn't burned off yet, so I headed to Stanley's for some breakfast.

As I ate I went through both morning papers. Burress wasn't dead, according to the *Morning Eagle*, but he was paralyzed on his right side and unable to speak, his active career at an end. The *Beacon* ignored it, though if they'd gotten wind of the presence of half-naked whores and sneaky photographers they certainly would have featured it as their lead. I wondered about sending the photo of Burress to Wilbur Lamarr and George Latham, just as a warning. I didn't think I needed to, though. With one member of their cabal in the ground and the other in intensive care, the message was probably getting through.

Even if it wasn't, I was done with the whole shutterbug angle anyway; it would be time for something more direct, so just for laughs I started thinking up ways Latham might get hurt. There was always the danger of something falling onto a man, for example. When I was still in England, a Master Sergeant in the Quartermaster Corps had gotten badly injured that way. An organized man with a knack for detail and a stick up his ass for proper procedure, the sarge had started investigating shortages in certain categories. Poor fellow was walking under a fourth-story window when a fifty-pound bag of cement toppled off the sill where someone had carelessly propped it. He was lucky, in a way, since he didn't die and got to go home years earlier than he would have, and no one in authority ever figured out who'd left the bag there. Or ever tried very hard, either.

There were ways to sabotage a car, too, though there was always the attendant risk of injuring bystanders, if that kind of thing bothered one. And of course there was my friend Rackey, who might do anything to a man he suspected of nailing his dear wife.

At eleven I met Wageknecht at the Personnel office. Whittaker seemed well-pleased for once, and I left them filling out paperwork and headed for the boss's office to tell him the good news.

Millie gave a little start at the sight of me, then with an insincere half-smile that was very unlike her she looked down and pretended to be looking for something in her desk drawer. "You can go right in, Mr. Ogden."

Collins was waiting for me, hands clasped behind his head. He looked confident to the point of arrogance, and healthier than I'd seen him look since before the war. "Ogden," he said as I sat on the corner of his desk.

"Found you a new bodyguard and driver."

"Did you."

"Wageknecht, the fellow who shot the dirty pictures of Huff."

"Good man. Resourceful. Glad you thought of that. And your timing is perfect. You know why? I was afraid I was going to have to do the hiring myself."

"How come?"

"Because I'm firing you, you dumb shit."

I wished the shovel from last night was in my hands right then. I'd have smashed the ungrateful bastard's face the way I'd done Ralph's. I didn't really care when he'd fired me drunk, but doing it sober was an unforgiveable insult. I had personally gotten this man free of a crippling addiction to narcotics, had risked imprisonment to safeguard his position at the company he founded, and had provided him with every vice imaginable, all the while serving as something almost like a friend, since Everett Collins had none left. If nothing else I was owed loyalty and gratitude.

"I wanted you to take care of a little problem with the board, not kill the sons of bitches one by one."

I maintained my calm in case the situation could be salvaged. "Burress isn't dead, sir, and Huff wasn't strictly a member of the board. Anyway, how do you know I had anything to do with Burress?"

"Are you fucking with me right now, boy?"

Every second that passed left me less interested in holding onto my position as his monkey. "Begging your pardon, Everett, but when I fuck with you, you'll know you've been fucked with."

His mutilated ear was redder than I'd ever seen it, and concentrating on that detail helped me maintain my equanimity in the face of the grizzled old sot's betrayal. "Did it occur to you," he said without moving his jaw, "that this might look bad in the eyes of the rest of the board? Of the shareholders? That somewhere down the line the police might get involved?"

"Why would the police get involved? Burress had a stroke. And I went into Huff's house the other night and stole the letter and the photograph."

"Don't try and confuse things, you devious son of a bitch. I been thinking about how ever since you got back from the war things have been going crazy around here. People killing themselves. Me getting stuck on that damned medicine and having to pay for a cure. Hiring whores for things besides fucking. And it always comes down to your doing. You weren't like that before the war, Ogden. I don't know what happened to you over there but I don't want it here any more."

A sudden wave of relief washed over me, and that urge to beat Collins to death with my bare hands evaporated. I was a free man; I saw the door to my own future open before me, inevitable. I was Saul of Tarsus on the road to Damascus. Though I didn't forgive him his treachery, the old man had unwittingly set me free to realize a better, more profitable destiny. "If that's the way you want it, Boss," I said.

"Hell yes that's the way I want it. And don't go thinking about trying to get me into trouble with what you know. Whittaker down in Personnel has a nice severance check waiting for you when you get done in here."

"That's all right. I'm sure I'll pick something else up."

"Not in the aircraft business you won't. I've spoken to every boss man in the industry, and you're blackballed, you son of a bitch. Now get out."

When I walked out, Wageknecht was speaking to Millie Grau. As soon as she saw me she pointed to the inner office and told him to go in. As soon as he was in there talking to my former employer she rose and, to my great surprise, embraced me.

"You're a good man, Wayne Ogden, and Mr. Collins is just dead wrong firing you."

"Thanks, Millie."

"It was that letter from Mr. Park."

"What, Herman Park? What kind of letter?"

She took a deep breath and looked at the floor. "Mr. Park came by with a letter addressed to Mr. Collins. He insisted on delivering it personally, and he stayed in there a good forty-five minutes. When he left Mr. Collins was hopping mad at you. I don't know what was said but it wasn't good."

"It's all right, kiddo. I'll land on my feet."

Walking out the front door of the office complex, without having stopped by Personnel to get that check, I reflected that Millie Grau, wonderful woman that she was, was nonetheless an abysmal judge of character.

I DIDN'T TELL Sally I'd been fired, but I did make a show out of reading aloud an ad in the *Morning Eagle* calling for vets to re-enlist. "I could be making good money back in the service," I said that evening as she attempted to knit a tiny hat for the baby.

"Better than at Collins?"

"No, but good money just the same."

"Huh. Well, as long as there isn't another war. I was awful worried about you the whole time you were gone."

"There won't be another war, baby."

The dinner she'd made was quite edible—canned peas, fried pork chops, and applesauce from a jar, and I hadn't had to pretend to enjoy it. The sincerity of my praise got me out of the house without having to weather any hysterics, and I drove out to Ebenezer Lutheran Church and parked on the street with the sun casting long shadows on the lush green lawns of east Wichita. For a few minutes I sat watching a building in the back of the church. These, according to Millie, were the quarters for unmarried clergy in which Donald would abide until his marriage in November. The others were empty at the moment.

After a few minutes' wait Donald walked out and headed up the sidewalk. I figured I had a good fifteen minutes and strolled around the block once and approached the building from the opposite side of the street. I pulled on the screen door and picked the cheap lock of the inner door with a bent paper clip.

It was spartan and dank inside, with a sour, sharp odor of mold emanating from carpet and furniture both. The kitchenette was filthy, and I wondered why the Lutherans, unlike the Catholics, didn't spring for housekeepers for their unmarried clergy. Several days' worth of dirty dishes sat in the sink, including a tumbler whose bottom third contained what appeared to be buttermilk. Milky, fetid water that smelled five feet away filled the rest of the glass.

I wasn't here to gather information on his homemaking skills, though. A man of thirty who's never married and doesn't fool around has got to have some method of disposing of his seminal backlog. It was possible that he frequented whores or had a secret along the line of Huff's, but that wasn't my impression. What I'd gathered about Donald made me think he was sexually stunted, what the shrinks call an arrested adolescent. In other words, a jerk-off artist. Something told me I'd find a secret stash of masturbatory aids somewhere within easy reach of the bed or the toilet. Since there was a Kleenex box right on the nightstand I decided to check under the bed first. Nothing but an empty mousetrap down there, but between the mattress and the box springs I hit paydirt: a stack of cheaply printed magazines and thirty-odd eight-by-ten glossies of the cheapest variety and lowest quality, mostly homely girls shyly smiling in their birthday suits. The magazines were of the cheesecake variety, bare tits and suggestive captions, but even still, nothing you want your pastor yanking his chain to.

I replaced all of it and went back out to the car to wait for his return. I hoped it would be soon, because I didn't want to wait for tomorrow to decide his fate. No, I didn't intend to convict him without a fair trial and a chance to defend himself.

Ten minutes later he came walking up the sidewalk, preoccupied and holding a grocery sack under his arm. I got out of the car and approached him as he unlatched a screen door.

He frowned. "Can I help you?"

Close up I could see he had some sort of skin condition. His face was inflamed from a recent shave, and his ears were vermillion like the boss's when he got drunk. Maybe that was the attraction for Millie. Maybe Donald was the result of one of those long-ago wayward nights in the old man's past. But I had business to attend to and no time for idle fancy.

"You Donald?"

"I am."

"My name's Ogden. Friend of your fiancé's."

"From work," he said, his nostrils flaring, though he showed no other outward sign of distaste.

"Right. Could I have a few minutes of your time?"

He let me in and I took a wooden chair without being invited to do so as he sat down on the reeking sofa.

"I just want to say it's real big of you to forgive her the way you did."

The look of confusion on his face as he pondered his options was pretty funny. Stand up and sock me in the jaw? Throw me out? Tell me it was none of my fucking business? Any or all of the three of those would have made him a man in my eyes, but he just leaned back with his arms folded across his chest.

Every syllable was clipped and precise, and after every two or three words came a little pause as he weighed the next. "It was a complicated situation. I'm aware that she confided in you before she did me, and that you advised her to tell me."

"No need to thank me, pal."

"I'm not thanking you. I would have much preferred to keep my mental image of her as pure and chaste."

At least now he was getting a little steamed. I wondered if I could get him to take a swing at me. "Sure, everybody wants to marry a virgin. But really, how many of us do? And even then it's over after the first time you top her. If you ask me that whole cherrybusting business is overrated."

"You miss the point entirely. I believed I was engaged to one kind of woman and I found myself engaged to another." He was talking faster but that prissy diction stayed with him, and I was thinking he must be a real snooze in the pulpit. "To a man like me the idea of coming to the marriage bed intact means a great deal, and when she told me the truth, I'll be quite honest with you, I called her a name and asked her to leave."

"Yeah? What name?"

He hesitated. "Slattern," he said with a little choke, as though it were the dirtiest word he knew, and I had to take in a deep breath in order not to snort. "I regretted it instantly, but in the heat of the moment one says hurtful things."

"So what made you decide she was worthy after all?"

"I don't see as that's any of your business."

Finally I'd coaxed a reaction out of this stiff that I could understand, an acknowledgment that it was shameful to be sitting here discussing his intimate personal life with a stranger. But my relief was short-lived.

"I'm glad to get it off my chest, to be honest. There's no one I can talk to about it. I can't tell the senior pastor, I don't want him looking at my wife that way. I can't tell my parents, they wouldn't understand." He looked like he was about to cry. If he did, I told myself, I'd knock his fucking block off. "I didn't decide she was worthy. I decided I couldn't call it off because people would ask questions. I'm a thirty-year-old associate pastor and I need to be married or it will seem odd. I need a wife and it might as well be her."

"You're a good egg," I said, standing up. "Millie's a lucky girl to have a fellow like you."

"Thanks," he said as I opened the door and let myself out.

Half an hour later I phoned Rackey's house. "It's Ogden."

"Heard you got fired, Mr. Ogden."

"It's all right, Rackey, I got some other things going on. But I need to warn you about something."

"Warn me?"

"I stood up to the old man the other morning and he couldn't take it, so he fired me. He may go after you next, see?"

"How come? Cause you hired me?"

"No, that's not it. What I stood up to him over had to do with a woman."

"You and him fighting over the same gal?"

"No. I told him he was a skunk for putting the meat to a married woman, and the wife of an employee yet."

"Whose wife?"

Jesus, Rackey was as dumb as a bag of hammers. I was going to have to spell it right out for him.

In the morning I paid a visit to Dr. Ezra Groff, who seemed not at all surprised to find me asking for another script for Hycodan.

"Sometimes those cures don't take. Most of the time, if you ask me. Patient's got to want to quit and they hardly ever do."

"I guess he's old enough to know what he wants."

"Yes, I suppose he is." He handed me the slip of paper and grinned, his teeth yellow as onions and brown at the roots. "Tell him not to forget me when I put in my bid for County Coroner."

"He won't forget you, doc."

At Union Station shortly afterward I sent a telegram to my old pal Lester in Japan: ON MY WAY STOP PREPARE TO PULL STRINGS STOP. I don't know what kind of crazy hours they keep over there but

I figured whatever strings he had to pull could be pulled after I'd signed up, so without giving myself a chance to change my mind I headed for the recruiting office on Douglas.

The place was empty when I walked in except for one lonely recruiting officer with an oddly orange complexion and little round ears that stuck out perpendicular to his head. "I want to re-up," I told him, and when I told him I was a Master Sergeant he looked like it was the only good news he'd had all day.

"Hell of a thing, the war's over but it's not like the world stopped turning. We're losing all kinds of good experienced men and our re-enlistment rates are just rotten. What's the army going to look like in five or ten years when we have to fight the Russkies?"

I had a feeling that one was probably going to be eight or ten big explosions, but it really didn't matter to me. I was a supply sergeant, and the fighting end of things wasn't within my purview.

LACKING AN OFFICE phone, and unable to make the call within earshot of Sally, I got a pocketful of change and stepped inside a phone booth in the back of Gessler's Drugstore on Douglas and told the operator to get me the Nonpareil Photographic Studio in Kansas City. When Tessler finally picked up he was wary of talking on the phone, but he thanked me for putting him in touch with Lester a few months back. "Your pal's been a real good customer," he said.

"Listen, Merle, I got a favor to ask. Want you to send a stack of the best stuff you have to an address here in Wichita with a letter attached."

"When you say best . . . "

"I mean worst. The stuff in the third folder."

He chuckled. "Oh, yeah, I got stuff'll make you puke."

"Perfect. You send those, without any return address on the envelope . . . "

"Come on, what do you take me for, stupid? I never use a return address."

"Good. Here's the letter you include, addressed to Donald Thorsten."

I recited slowly enough for him to take it down: "'Dear Don, Had a bit of a hard time tracking you down after you left Grand Rapids. I hear Wichita is a wide open town so enjoy yourself. Here's the new set, I hope one or all will be to your liking. Please remember that you have a credit of seven dollars fifty-two cents on your account. Best wishes, D.R. McMillan. P.S. I hear you're getting married, congratulations. Hope she knows what she's getting into and you too (ha ha).'" I listened while he scratched down the last few words. "Got that?"

He said he thought he did and then read it back to me. "Where do I send this?"

"Ebenezer Lutheran Church in Wichita." I recited the address and had him read it back to me.

"Care of this Donald Thorsten character?" he said.

"No. The envelope is just addressed to the church. I want one of the church secretaries to open it first."

"Jesus. Some poor old Lutheran lady is going to have a rude fucking awakening." He laughed. I did, too, since the image of the church secretary's face as she opened the envelope and got a load of some broad fucking a Rottweiler hadn't previously entered my mind.

"Can't be helped," I said. "What am I going to owe you for the pictures?"

"On the house. You got me some decent business; it's my pleasure to return the favor."

SIXTEEN

PACIFICATION

THE REPLY TO my telegram came quickly, and I pulled it out of my pocket like a winning lottery ticket:

CONSIDER STRINGS PULLED STOP WELCOME
BACK STOP TOLD GALS TO GET READY STOP

Now that my leaving was official, I was amazed that I'd held out this long in Wichita.

I left with no qualms or regrets; I was doing the right thing by my wife and child; as a Master Sergeant stationed outside the U.S. I'd be making nearly two hundred dollars a month base pay. Given whatever Lester and I could scrape together on the black market and on the backs of the Japanese lovelies—who would be serving our country just as much as we were—I could easily send the whole two hundred home to Sally and the child plus something on the side.

The scene Sally made when I told her I was heading for Japan was worse than I'd anticipated. When I'd talked about re-enlisting she'd pictured me stationed somewhere in the U.S., living off base with her and the kid. I'd married a woman with a real backbone, and I felt a kind of pride when she threw a carving knife at me, taking a gash out of the doorframe.

"You son of a bitch, where do you get off walking out on me with a baby on the way? How'm I supposed to take care of the damned thing on my own?"

I'd prepared a cornball lecture on the evils of the commie threat and the need to keep Japan pacified and a whole load of other crap, which I delivered between bouts of screaming and more thrown household goods, including two ashtrays, a rolling pin (shades, again, of Maggie and Jiggs), and a pretty good clock we'd received as a wedding present from a cousin of mine in California. In the end she locked herself in the bedroom and I left the house to let her cool off.

THE DAY BEFORE I left Wichita I drove up to the plant gates with some trepidation. My badge was no longer valid, and I was by no means certain that the guard would let me pass. But I wanted to get my framed photo of the hissing opossum off of my office wall, and there were a couple of people I wanted to say goodbye to. And of course I hadn't yet bothered returning the company Oldsmobile.

The guard was Jerry something, an old-timer who'd been with Everett Collins since his barnstorming days. Jerry grinned and waved me past like an old friend.

The other fellows in the publicity and marketing department didn't bother to hide their satisfaction at my fate. Mrs. Caspian gave me a sad look but said nothing except "good luck." I took one last look at her belly and tossed her a casual, backward wave on my way out the door.

Millie Grau was bravely manning her post at the entry to Everett Collins's empty office, and she looked as though she'd been awake for a week. Her eyes were dry but there was a deep sadness in her face and voice that I supposed I might be partially responsible for.

"Mr. Ogden. It's nice to see you," she said.

"Call me Wayne, I don't work here any more. What do you hear about the old man?"

"Still in serious condition, don't know when he'll be out. Lots of physical therapy, maybe some more surgeries."

"So Rackey just busted in here and started whaling on him?"

She nodded; clearly this was a hard memory to revisit. "He was screaming about his wife and Mr. Collins being . . . intimate, and it took four men to subdue him. Three of them went to the hospital, too."

I was proud of Rackey; he'd bested his own casualty record from his arrest by the MPs. "Can I go in there and leave him a little note?"

"Oh, I'll be at the hospital this afternoon, I can take it to him."

"I'd rather he found it when he's feeling a little better, after he's had some time to think things through. Something to let him know I still admire and respect him."

"That will mean the world to him, Wayne. You know, I'm pretty sure once he's feeling better he'll wish he hadn't fired you," she said.

"It's for the best," I said, and without waiting for further permission I opened the door to his office. It was dark and eerie, with the same unoccupied smell as an empty hotel room, and I felt the way I did breaking into Huff's house. I opened up a side drawer and gently placed the dark brown glass pill bottle into it. He was bound to be hurting still when he returned from the hospital, and two hundred hits of Hycodan would be a good way for me to say "No hard feelings, boss."

Outside I found Millie brewing coffee. "If you have time," she said, flashing a wan smile at me.

WE WERE SILENT until the coffee was ready, and after she poured it she gave me an even sadder look than she'd worn when I walked in. "I sure was sorry to hear you were joining the army."

"It's a good deal they give returning NCOs."

"I mean I was sure hoping you'd come back to work. Things have been pretty rotten here lately."

"You'll be getting married in a few months."

She shook her head and looked at the ceiling. "Donald had some trouble with the church and lost his job, and between you and me . . . " She looked away from me, not quite able to give me the sad news about Donald's twisted hobbies.

"You don't have to tell me."

"Anyway I won't be marrying him."

I looked at her and wished I could tell her what I'd done, but in these cases women weren't necessarily rational, and you never knew if she'd be grateful or angry. Once again I was seized with admiration and desire for her, and a crazy thought came into my head. I decided to act on it, knowing that I'd always regret not trying.

"Millie, have you ever thought about leaving here?"

"Lately? You bet. Where would I go, though? I can't go back to Wisconsin. I don't know anyone anywhere else."

"Sure you do. The army has civilian employees, and you're a crackerjack secretary. I'm going back into the Quartermaster Corps, in occupied Japan, and I have a friend who could fix it for you. I could get you assigned to my unit, probably."

She stared at me for a moment as though seriously considering it, and then another look crossed her face, one that suggested she understood to some degree the nature of my proposition, was maybe even beginning to understand that I was the one who'd saved her from Donald. Whatever was going on in that pretty blonde head, she looked a little bit nauseous.

"Mr. Ogden . . . "

"Wayne," I said, smiling my most charming smile.

"Wayne, I'm very dedicated to my job here with Mr. Collins, and I don't think I care to change anything."

"Understood," I said. "Just something that popped into my head."

"I have a lot of work to do now." She was smiling, too, tense and insincere. "It's been nice catching up."

I stared her down until she looked away and started digging into a drawer as an excuse to ignore me, then I wished her luck and walked out the door. Too bad she was too scared to jump when the jumping was good; I was still glad I'd helped her out, but from here on out she was on her own. I was done playing Good Samaritan for people who didn't give a damn one way or the other about it.

Miss Grau no longer bore contemplation, anyway; she belonged to Wichita, part of a past that as of tomorrow I would no longer acknowledge as my own. Along with my father's armchair, Norman's blind pig, and my various heirs *in utero*, I would abandon her permanently, to be remembered in tranquility and without undue nostalgia.

I DROVE OFF the plant grounds in the company Olds with the thought that this was my last night in Wichita—maybe ever—elating me to the point of dizziness, despite a sneaking fondness for certain of the town's darker corners.

On East Douglas I passed the spot just west of the Uptown Theater where I'd once burned a car right down to its frame, an image I'd almost forgotten and one that brought an unabashed smile. On a whim I turned right onto Hillside and right again onto First, past a stately columned home where I'd gotten a plump, pretty housewife half-naked before her husband came home and chased me out the back door waving a knife. I was seventeen then, and until today it had never occurred to me to wonder what effect that episode had had on their lives. In another house on the same street my friend Don Milligan used to live with his folks until he crashed his Willys into a milk truck, killing himself and the milkman, having just let me off at my house after a night of drinking. Most of these blocks had some story attached to them in my memory, and though it was unlikely I'd ever be back to see them again I felt no sense of loss. The stories would stick with me.

I'd have dinner with Sally tonight, of course, and for decency's sake swing by my mother's to say goodbye. Later I might head downtown to the Eaton for one last party with Irma, maybe take her over to Norman's afterward and make him a gift of her company for the rest of the night; he'd certainly poured me enough free drinks over the years.

A YEAR WASTED on civilian life had brought me nothing but boredom relieved occasionally by frenzy and mayhem as I clung tight to the miserable delusion that life as a husband, father, and citizen was my inevitable fate. Now the scales had fallen from my eyes to reveal a destiny worthy of my talents. Japan and Mother Army beckoned like a pair of madams at the door of the world's biggest, best cathouse, and I was on my way there to play piano in the parlor.